CHERRY AMES CRUISE NURSE

By

HELEN WELLS

SPRINGER PUBLISHING COMPANY
New York

Copyright © 1948 by Grosset & Dunlap, Inc.
Copyright © renewed 2007 by Harriet Schulman Forman
Springer Publishing Company, LLC

Springer Publishing Company, LLC
11 West 42nd Street
New York, NY 10036-8002
www.springerpub.com

Acquisitions Editor: Sally J. Barhydt
Series Editor: Harriet S. Forman
Production Editor: Carol Cain
Cover design: Takeout Graphics, Inc.
Composition: Apex Publishing, LLC

07   08   09   10/   5   4   3   2

Library of Congress Cataloging-in-Publication Data

Wells, Helen.
    Cherry Ames, cruise nurse / by Helen Wells.
      p. cm. — (Cherry Ames nurse stories)
    Summary: Looking forward to a working vacation as nurse on a cruise ship to the Caribbean, Cherry Ames soon finds herself embroiled in a dangerous mystery involving a sickly child and greedy men anxious to find a secret stockpile of precious ambergris.
    ISBN-13: 978-0-8261-0411-3 (alk. paper)
    ISBN-10: 0-8261-0411-8 (alk. paper)
  [1. Nurses—Fiction.   2. Ocean travel—Fiction.   3. Interpersonal relations—Fiction.   4. Mystery and detective stories.]   I. Title.
PZ7.W4644Cde   2007
[Fic]—dc22   2007016206

Printed in the United States of America by Bang Printing

Contents

~~~~~~

iv CONTENTS

Foreword

~~~~~~

Helen Wells, the author of the Cherry Ames stories, said, "I've always thought of nursing, and perhaps you have, too, as just about the most exciting, important, and rewarding profession there is. Can you think of any other skill that is *always* needed by everybody, everywhere?"

I was and still am a fan of Cherry Ames. Her courageous dedication to her patients; her exciting escapades; her thirst for knowledge; her intelligent application of her nursing skills; and the respect she achieved as a registered nurse (RN) all made it clear to me that I was going to follow in her footsteps and become a nurse—nothing else would do. Thousands of other young readers were motivated by Cherry Ames to become RNs as well. Through her thought-provoking stories, Cherry Ames led a steady stream of students into schools of nursing across the country well into the 1960s and 1970s when the series ended.

Readers who remember enjoying these books in the past will take pleasure in reading them again now—whether or not they chose nursing as their life's work.

Perhaps they will share them with others and even motivate a person or two to choose nursing as a career path.

My nursing path has been rich and satisfying. I have
delivered babies, cared for people in hospitals and
in their homes, and saved lives. I have worked at the
bedside and served as an administrator, I have published
journals, written articles, taught students, consulted, and
given expert testimony. Never once did I regret my deci-
sion to become a nurse.

During the time that I was publishing a nursing jour-
nal, I became acquainted with Robert Wells, brother
of Helen Wells. In the course of conversation I learned
that Ms. Wells had passed on and left the Cherry Ames
copyright to Mr. Wells. Because there is a shortage of
nurses here in the US today, I thought, "Why not bring
Cherry back to motivate a whole new generation of
young people? Why not ask Mr. Wells for the copyright
to Cherry Ames?" Mr. Wells agreed, and the republished
series is dedicated both to Helen Wells, the original author, and to her brother, Robert Wells, who transferred
the rights to me. I am proud to ensure the continuation
of Cherry Ames into the twenty-first century.

The final dedication is to you, both new and old
readers of Cherry Ames: It is my dream that you enjoy
Cherry's nursing skills as well as her escapades. I
hope that young readers will feel motivated to choose
nursing as their life's work. Remember, as Helen Wells
herself said: there's no other skill that's "*always* needed
by everybody, everywhere."

Harriet Schulman Forman, RN, EdD
Series Editor

CHAPTER I

Waiting for a Letter

CHERRY OPENED ONE DARK-BROWN EYE AND CLOSED IT again quickly. Shivering, she pulled the covers up until her black curls were hidden beneath the thick, crazy-quilt comforter.

Cherry had been dreaming. It was such a very pleasant dream she didn't want to stop. She was dreaming that she was back in her own room in Hilton, Illinois. She had cautiously opened one eye to make sure everything was exactly the same in the dream as it was in real life:

Her dressing table with its dotted-swiss skirts and brisk red bows; the crisp, ruffled white curtains tied back with bright-red ribbon; a stream of cold December sunlight pouring through the open window to bring out the varied colors in the hooked rug her grandmother had made.

Cherry sighed. If only the dream could come true. But, of course, she wasn't home. She was with the rest of the Spencer Club in Greenwich Village, New York City.

For one year and three months now Cherry had been a visiting nurse, sharing No. 9, the Greenwich Village apartment, with Josie, Gwen, Bertha, Vivian, and Mai Lee. They were all visiting nurses too. Thinking about the Spencer Club made Cherry realize more than ever that she must be dreaming. If she were awake she would hear them chattering as they dressed and breakfasted.

No one could sleep through the chatter and the clatter and confusion of an early working-day morning in No. 9. You couldn't even dream through it, Cherry decided, and boldly opened both eyes. She sniffed tentatively.

The crisp, cold air was laden with the delicious blend of freshly perked coffee and thick slabs of bacon frying on the stove in her mother's kitchen. Cherry pinched one red cheek and then the other. She was awake. She wasn't dreaming! She was *home!*

And then it all came back to her. She remembered that two weeks ago the dizziness had suddenly gotten worse; so much worse that everything went black for a minute. The dizzy spells, she had known for a long time, were due to fatigue.

Cherry had been making a report about a contagious disease that had suddenly broken out in her district:

Mumps—nothing very serious, but should they try the new inoculation?

"The Lerner children are all down with it," Cherry was stuttering. Her tongue felt thick and dry in her mouth. Her head ached. Her back ached. Her legs ached from knee to toe. Her feet were weighted down with the iron clamps of complete exhaustion.

She stared across the desk, trying to focus her eyes on Miss Dorothy Davis, her supervisor. And then all of a sudden Miss Davis's face began to dance and whirl. Nausea flooded over Cherry. She gripped the edge of the desk with sweating fingers. *She wasn't going to faint.* Nurses don't go around fainting. Nurses can't even spare the time to be sick. Not when they know that in one year in New York City alone the Visiting Nurse Service gave nursing care to almost five million people!

But Cherry did faint. Everything went black for a minute. When she came to, Miss Davis had pushed Cherry's head down between her knees. Now she handed Cherry a glass of water into which she had stirred a teaspoon of aromatic spirits of ammonia.

"Drink up," Miss Davis said briskly. "You're going to be all right, Ames. You're overtired. Need a vacation. Take your work too seriously."

Cherry drank up and felt better. The dizziness ebbed away, but the ache had spread to every bone and joint in her body. She struggled to her feet. Miss Davis tucked Cherry's hand in the crook of her arm.

"I'm sending you home in a cab," she said. "A relief nurse will cover your district while you're gone. And you're going to be gone for one whole month."

"Oh, no, please," Cherry had protested weakly. "Mr. Morvell . . . Mrs. di Pattio . . . the Lerner children—"

The supervisor snapped her fingers, her brown eyes flashing. But her smile was warm. "Listen to me, Cherry Ames. You're not the only visiting nurse in the world. Run-down and exhausted as you are, you're not really much good to us. You're a liability right now." She grinned to take the edge off her words. "A month's leave of absence and you're an asset again. We need assets. Your boss's orders. See?"

Cherry had managed a sickly laugh. "Yes, ma'am, but—"

And then Mrs. Berkey, the assistant supervisor, appeared on the scene. She was tall and capable looking, and her gray eyes were grim. "I'm taking you home, Ames," she said. "Now. Have an errand downtown anyway. Cab's waiting. Hustle into your coat and rubbers. I'm a busy woman."

Cherry meekly obeyed. Orders were orders. She was too weary to argue further anyway.

Outside in the street, Mrs. Berkey, holding Cherry firmly by the arm as they walked toward a waiting cab, said, "Miss Davis and I have had our eyes on you for the past month. You need a good long rest. *And* a change."

During the ride downtown Mrs. Berkey had said something else which even now Cherry couldn't quite believe. She'd said that what Cherry needed was a Caribbean cruise. Miss Davis was going to try to arrange it. Her brother, Dr. Fowler Davis, was in the medical department of one of the big steamship lines.

There was, however, a long waiting list. Cruise jobs were prized by nurses, exhausted by long hours and understaffed hospitals. But Cherry, Mrs. Berkey said, should spend a couple of weeks at home before taking on any new duties anyway. And then it would be the holiday season. A great many nurses on the list might withdraw their names, preferring to spend Christmas at home . . .

Cherry sat up in bed and tugged the comforter around her shoulders. It was too good to come true. A Caribbean cruise! The round trip would take twelve days. Almost two weeks of warm weather and sea air. A stopover at the exciting-sounding island of Curaçao in the Netherlands West Indies; then on to Venezuela and Colombia in South America.

But there was a long waiting list. That, Cherry decided, was the catch. There must be hundreds of other overtired young nurses ahead of her on the list. They must have signed up ages ago for ship's-nurse jobs on luxury ocean liners cruising to glamorous Caribbean ports. What chance did Ames have?

Ames, Cherry admitted ruefully, had waited too long. She had known a month ago that she was suffering from fatigue and needed a vacation, if not a change.

"I was silly," Cherry scolded herself now. "As Miss Davis said, I'm not the only visiting nurse in the world."

Well, she had learned her lesson. She had been relaxing now for almost two weeks and felt fine. But it still seemed like a dream to be home.

Breakfast in bed. Window-shopping with Midge, home too, for the holidays. Long, satisfying talks with Midge's father, Dr. Joe. And best of all, wonderful, quiet evenings around the fire with her mother and father. They talked very little as they munched buttered popcorn and lazily cracked nuts, watching the smoldering logs crumple into dying embers. But the very peace and quiet of those happy evenings had gradually stopped the dull ache in her tired body. And now that Charlie was home on vacation too, life was perfect.

"In bed from nine to noon," Dr. Joseph Fortune had ordered, affectionately stern. He had ushered Cherry and her twin brother, Charlie, into the world. It was Dr. Joe who had inspired her to become a nurse.

Dear Dr. Joe with his beautiful, sensitive face and luminous eyes! "He was really worried about me when I tottered off the train and practically collapsed into Dad's arms."

Charlie had been worried too, Cherry knew; almost as upset as her parents had been, although she had gained back a few pounds before his arrival. But he hid his anxiety under a steady stream of teasing:

"If you don't get those red cheeks back soon, Nurse Ames, we'll have to change your name to Lily."

Charlie was the only one to whom Cherry had confided her dream of a Caribbean cruise. Cherry felt certain that her parents and Dr. Joe would have strenuous objections if she so much as mentioned it. It would be hard to convince them that she was well and strong now; that the trip actually would be good for her.

But Charlie understood. Charlie was as fair as his twin was dark, but they both had the same pert features. And Charlie was as much in love with preparing for his engineering career as Cherry had been with hers.

"Of course, nothing may come of it," Cherry had told him one night as they crunched through the snow on their way home from an early movie. "But I can dream, can't I? A ship's nurse on a luxury liner complete with swimming pool! You and Dad shoveling snow while I'm taking sun baths on the promenade deck."

"Wait a minute!" Charlie had stopped and swung her around so fast that her overshoes skidded on an icy patch in the sidewalk. "Let me get this straight. Are you working your way to South America or going as a passenger?"

Cherry giggled. "Both. I understand the work's not too hard except when there's an epidemic of seasickness or an emergency of some sort. Besides, I like to work. I'd be bored to death lying in the sun and dunking myself in the pool all day long."

Charlie chuckled. "You'll run into seasickness, honey, the first night out. But good. Rough seas when you hit the Gulf Stream around Cape Hatteras. Wouldn't be surprised if you landed in sick bay yourself."

Cherry pretended to pout. "You're just jealous, you landlubber you!"

"Seriously, honey, it's a wonderful idea. I hope you get the job. You deserve it, and the change will fix you right up. You'll be as good as new when you come back; fat and brown with those fabulous red cheeks of yours."

"Keep your fingers crossed, Charlie, please." Cherry had tucked her arm affectionately through his. "There's a long waiting list."

There it was again. That disheartening little phrase: just three simple words, "Long waiting list!"

Now Cherry jumped out of bed, closed the window, and popped into the warmth of the bathroom to brush her teeth and dash icy cold water into her face, "I won't think about it any more," she resolutely mumbled into the towel. "I'm almost halfway through my month's vacation now. If word doesn't come soon I wouldn't be able to take the job anyway."

She snatched up a warm bed jacket of quilted blue silk and hopped hack into bed, obeying Dr. Joe's orders to the letter. Then counting on her fingers she said out loud:

"I've already had twelve days. The round-trip cruise is another twelve days. Twelve and twelve make twenty-four. One month is four weeks. There are twenty-eight days in four weeks . . ."

There was a knock on her door. It opened a crack. Midge's face appeared. "Talking to herself. That means money in the bank. Or that she's losing her mind."

After Midge's face came the rest of her; or at least what you could see behind the enormous breakfast tray she was carrying.

"Good morning, Miss Fortune," Cherry greeted her teen-age neighbor, Dr. Joe's mischievous daughter. "Since when did you start specialing me?" She crossed her legs under her and reached out hungrily for the tray.

Midge sniffed. "Specialing indeed. I'm not your private duty nurse. I'm your mother's helper, that's all." She curled up at the foot of the bed adding, *"And* my father's private detective. I'm to sit right here and see that you eat every morsel on the tray. Even that burnt crust on the toast I made."

Cherry gratefully gulped down a large glass of fresh orange juice. "There's my vitamin C for the day. And I *like* burnt toast. Especially when you can coat it with sweet butter and homemade strawberry jam." She sighed in ecstasy. "Did you scramble these delicious, fluffy eggs, Midge Fortune?"

It was, of course, a rhetorical question. Midge didn't bother to answer. It was an accepted fact in Hilton that harum-scarum Midge was about as domestically inclined as a longshoreman.

After Dr. Fortune's wife died, Midge had tried in her own way to keep house for him between school and mischievous pranks. But her own way was so topsy-turvy that Dr. Joe might have become anemic if he hadn't been frequently invited to supper by Mrs. Ames. Cherry herself had often swept and dusted the Fortune house; made beds, seen to it that the kitchen cupboards and the refrigerator were stocked with easy-to-prepare but vitamin- and mineral-packed meals.

"It's wonderful to be home," Cherry said, completely dismissing her dream of a Caribbean cruise. "I'm just beginning to realize how much I missed you all. As Gwen kept saying, 'Life in Greenwich Village is glamorous and exciting,' but—but . . ." She nibbled thoughtfully on a piece of bacon. "I guess I'm pretty much of a homebody in spite of all my wanderings."

Midge stared at her in disgust. "You make me tired, Cherry Ames. I can't imagine anything more wonderful than a Bohemian apartment in Greenwich Village. Complete with garden."

"Garden?" Cherry shook back her thick, dark curls, laughing. "Bertha Larsen said it was so small the chickens on her farm would have ignored it. But last summer we did finally make a little bower out of that tiny, fenced-in back yard. Nasturtiums—"

"Nasty urchins, you mean," Midge corrected her with a giggle. "That's what I called 'em until I grew up."

Cherry ignored this golden opportunity to point out to Midge that she was still far from grown up. "Heavenly blue morning-glories all over the fence," she went on reminiscently. "And in the fall we even coaxed a few marigolds into blooming. Mai Lee has a green thumb with flowers."

Suddenly Cherry was homesick for the Spencer Club and its headquarters in downtown New York. It was only a passing, although poignant, longing, but for a moment she stared unseeingly down at her empty plate.

They were all busy with their districts while she sat here in bed, doing nobody any good and probably causing the whole household unnecessary trouble.

"Completely silly, this business of breakfast in bed," she told Midge grimly. "Because I'm all better now. Really and truly I am. I don't need a whole month of this petting and spoiling. Ten days just being *home* has done the trick. I must get back to work."

But Midge wasn't listening. "All the celebrities you met in Greenwich Village," she was saying enviously. "Tell me again, Cherry, about the Indian woman who wanders around swathed in veils. And the barefoot, bearded man in the flowing, white toga."

"It's not those people I miss," Cherry said under her breath. "It's the people who need me; my district families. But Dorothy Davis said I couldn't come back until my month was up. Oh, how I wish I dared hope I'd get a letter from the steamship line today!"

She clapped her hand over her mouth too late. She didn't want Midge or anybody else, except Charlie, to know anything about her dream of a ship's-nurse job; at least not until everything was settled. *If* there was such a thing as a dream coming true.

She glanced sharply at Midge. Had she heard what Cherry had muttered about a steamship line?

Midge either hadn't heard or was pretending she hadn't heard. She was staring unconcernedly up at the ceiling.

"Have you thought about what you want for Christmas, Cherry?" Midge asked. "There's no sense in asking you what you want for your birthday. People who have birthdays the day before Christmas are out of luck so far as I'm concerned. It must be awful having them come so close together."

"It isn't awful at all." Cherry laughed. "It's fun celebrating two days in a row. And, no, I haven't thought about what I want for either Christmas or my birthday. Any suggestions?"

Midge, still staring up at the ceiling, said, "Next Monday, a week from today, is Chrismas. You'd better write a letter to Santa Claus. But quick."

Cherry lowered the tray to the floor. She relaxed against the pillows thinking:

"I know what I want for my birthday. *And* Christmas. A letter from that nice Dr. Davis who interviewed me before I left New York. A letter on the exciting-looking, glamorous, steamship line's stationery. A letter saying that one Cherry Ames has been hired as ship's nurse for the duration of a twelve-day cruise."

She closed her eyes and let her imagination carry her away. The Caribbean! Buccaneers. Pirates. The Spanish Main, Christmas on the high seas. That meant Christmas without Mother and Dad and Charlie. A lump swelled in Cherry's throat. Then she sat up, laughing at herself:

"Here I am getting homesick while I'm still at home! There's not a chance in the world that long waiting list has dwindled down to my size."

"I wouldn't be too sure of that." It was Midge's voice, elaborately disinterested.

Cherry's black eyes popped wide open. "Midge! You know something I don't know."

Midge pursed her lips and whistled a bar or two of "Anchors Aweigh." Then she said, "The only thing I *know* is what I just happened to hear you say to Charlie last evening."

Cherry gasped. "What did I say?"

"You said, 'Oh, Charlie, do you think I have a chance?' And Charlie said: 'I feel it in my bones, honey. You'd better go shopping for whatever feminine gear a cruise nurse needs in the Caribbean.'"

"Midge Fortune!" Cherry's mother appeared in the doorway, mildly scolding. "What do you mean by sitting on Cherry's mail? I told you to let her read it in peace over breakfast!"

Mail! Cherry sucked in a deep breath. *Mail!*

Midge slid to the floor, dragging half the comforter with her. "Nothing but a silly old ad from a steamship company. I was going to throw it away."

But Cherry had already pounced on the long, flag-bedecked envelope. It was addressed to Miss Cherry Ames, R.N. Neatly typed above the row of tiny United States and South American flags in the upper left-hand corner was the name:

"Dr. Fowler Davis, Medical Department."

CHAPTER II

"Bon Voyage!"

CHERRY READ THE LETTER FROM DR. DAVIS FOR THE SEC-
ond time—out loud. She felt like laughing and crying
at once and her voice was so shaky she had to read it for
the third time before Mrs. Ames finally understood.

The nurse who had been engaged to sail aboard
the *Julita* on December twenty-second had suddenly
been taken ill. The applicants ahead of Cherry on
the list had withdrawn their names for the duration
of the holidays. Dr. Davis was taking Cherry's acceptance for granted—unless she wired him to the
contrary.

Cherry looked up from the letter and waited for the
verdict. Would her mother he overwhelmingly disappointed because Cherry was not going to be home for
Christmas after all? Would she call in Dr. Joe? Would
they all insist she was not yet strong enough to go back
on duty?

14

Cherry held her breath. The ship would sail at noon, Friday, December twenty-second! Four days and a few hours from this very minute. That left her hardly time enough to get her clothes and uniforms together and catch the first train to New York! The letter had said she was to report for instructions to the secretary of the medical department on Wednesday afternoon if possible. The *Julita* was due in from its twelve-day cruise that morning. She would probably have an opportunity to meet the ship's doctor Wednesday afternoon at the steamship line's offices on the pier. She must wire her acceptance at once.

Cherry's mind raced ahead. She hadn't done a bit of Christmas shopping yet. She could do that in New York Wednesday morning and all day Thursday. She ought to be calling about trains and making reservations now, sending a telegram to the Spencer Club. The room she shared with Gwen would be waiting for her. And that reminded Cherry that she must pay her share of the January rent before sailing, just in case the *Julita* was delayed by bad weather.

Tears filmed her eyes. Half of her wanted to go; the other half wanted to stay right here in Hilton. Through a blur she saw her mother's face, smiling down at her.

"Why, Cherry darling," Mrs. Ames was saying with just a suspicion of a catch in her voice. "It's wonderful! The very thing. Dr. Joe and I were saying only yesterday that you need a change and a dose of good, hot sun. We thought of Florida. But this is much better. Your father and Charlie will be so happy for you."

Cherry was out of bed, scrambling through tangled sheets and blankets to throw her arms around her mother. "Oh, Mrs. Ames, ma'am," she laughed and cried at once. "You're just about the understandingest mother a registered nurse ever had!"

The rest of the morning was a dizzy whirl of excitement. Dad came home for lunch with the train and Pullman tickets in his pocket. "Cherry Ames, Ship's Nurse!" He gave her a mock salute.

Charlie nagged her constantly with useless instructions. "Don't forget, honey, from now on stairs are ladders, floors are decks, beds are bunks—"

"Oh, stop it, Charlie!" Cherry clapped her hand lightly over his mouth. "The *Julita* is a luxury liner, not a transport or a destroyer. It's a house, I'll have you know. A mansion, I mean. Dr. Davis showed me pictures and a deck plan of her sister ship when he interviewed me two weeks ago. They have windows, not portholes; a dining *room,* a living *room,* and a library. Even a night club that opens onto a veranda above the swimming pool."

Charlie tugged at his blond hair in mock bewilderment. "Doesn't sound very nautical to me." He hopped around the room in a very bad imitation of a sailor's hornpipe.

Midge began to chant to the tune of "The Farmer in the Dell":

> *"Cherry's going to sea,*
> *Cherry's going to sea,*
> *Heigh-ho, the Cherrio,*
> *Cherry's going to sea!"*

Charlie topped it off with a hastily improvised ballad on the dangers of the pirate-infested Caribbean. He brought in Captain Kidd, Drake, and Morgan, and ended with Cherry walking the plank by order of Long John Silver.

What seemed like minutes later, Cherry was tensely trying to go to sleep in an upper berth of a streamliner speeding to New York. The night was endless, but the next day passed all too quickly.

She had hardly made out her Christmas shopping list and gathered her scattered thoughts when she found herself in the dim hallway of the Greenwich Village apartment house. Good old No. 9! Tacked in a row beside the doorbell were the Spencer Club's professional cards: Gwen's, Vivi's, Bertha's, Josie's, Mai Lee's and, last but not least, a faintly dusty one on which were engraved the words:

CHERRY AMES, R.N.

Cherry was tempted. None of them would be home until after six. It was hardly five-thirty now. None of them had had the faintest hint of her new job. Why not give them the surprise of their young lives?

She set down her suitcase and scrabbled through her wallet for a fresh card. Under her name she carefully added in bold, block printing, "Ship's Nurse." Giggling, she substituted the new card for the old one. That would give them a jolt. Gwen's eyes would bug right out of her head.

Cherry unlocked the blue door and slipped into the ground-floor apartment. The living room with the gold-and-white sprigged wallpaper looked just the same: Tidy, but not too tidy, with a pleasant, lived-in look. There were ashes under a huge, half-burnt log in the handsome fireplace. Books and magazines overflowed from the low shelves under the windows facing the street. The gold gauze curtains they had all helped make had a freshly laundered crispness.

"I'll bet Bertha did that." Cherry smiled to herself and went down the hall to the bedroom she shared with Gwen. Slowly she unpacked the few things she would need before sailing.

It seemed strange to be the only one home. And it seemed much stranger not to be tired and harried at the end of a working day. Luxuriating in the peace and quiet of the normally hectic apartment, she donned a warm flannel housecoat and bunny-toed scuffs. It was so cold she could see her breath. That janitor! He insisted too much heat was unhealthy.

In the tiny kitchenette Cherry fixed herself a cup of scalding tea and two thick slices of cinnamon toast. Munching between sips she wandered into the back parlor. She laughed as the sight of the blue furniture reminded her of that scrape. Another "Ames Folly," that one. The janitor had been furious when he discovered that the girls, at Cherry's suggestion, had painted the dingy chairs, table, and sideboard without his permission. But it had all ended happily.

Cherry heard the rattle of a key in the front door lock. Quickly she dumped her cup and saucer in the sink and hurried down the hall. It was red-haired Gwen with a smudge of subway soot on the end of her pert, freckled nose.

"Cherry Ames!"

"Gwenthyan Jones!"

Sturdy arms hugged Cherry tightly. "We got your wire, but we didn't believe a word of it. What gives? Why come back with Christmas less than a week away?"

"Oh, dear," Cherry moaned inwardly. "She didn't even notice my new card. What a fine jolt that turned out to be."

She opened her mouth to explain and then Bertha arrived, laden down with bundles of groceries. After that, Mai Lee showed up with Vivian right on her heels. Everybody talked at once, bombarding Cherry with questions. There was such a babel of voices that Cherry's replies were drowned out. And suddenly there was Josie, blinking bewilderedly behind her glasses.

"Cherry," she blurted in her rabbity way. She was holding Cherry's new card in one gloved hand. "What's this about you being a ship's nurse? Are you going to give up your district?"

"Ship's nurse," the others shouted in unison. "Who's a ship's nurse? Ames, you fiend! You've been holding out on us!"

Cherry backed away from them, stumbled, and sat down hard on the sofa, minus one scuff. They crowded around her excitedly, Mai Lee curling up on the worn carpet at her feet.

Bertha came to the rescue. "Girls, girls! Let her get her breath. Gwen, build a fire while I put the perishables in the icebox. They'll freeze in here if I don't." She bustled out to the kitchenette.

Gwen grumbled but went to work with crushed paper and kindling. Soon the log was blazing cheerily. Bertha came back with six cups of steaming hot tomato juice on a tray.

"Now," she said, settling her plump body in a chair. "Begin at the beginning, Cherry."

Cherry told them the whole thrilling story, apologizing, "I didn't know myself until I got Dr. Davis's letter yesterday morning. I didn't even give Mother a hint. I honestly didn't think I had a chance."

"Oh, Cherry, it's too good to be true!" Vivian's soft hazel eyes were wide with enthusiasm.

Cherry felt a twinge of remorse. Vivian needed a rest and change as much as Cherry did, but there was not a trace of envy in her warm smile.

"It's just what the doctor ordered, Cherry," Josie laughed.

"You lucky, lucky girl," Gwen shouted excitedly.

"I'm so glad for you, Cherry." Mai Lee quietly clapped her small ivory hands in approval. "You deserve it."

"I should say she does," Bertha Larsen cried emphatically. "I only hope they don't work you to death. Oh, my aching feet. At least you won't have to climb umpteen flights of stairs every day."

Cherry's black eyes twinkled. "You wouldn't swap jobs with me for anything, Bertha, and you know it.

You're in love with your district. All of you are. I miss my own patients so, sometimes I ache all over."

"A different kind of ache from mine," Gwen sniffed, rubbing her ankles as she toasted her stockinged feet in front of the fire. "Me, I'm so jealous I'm green. A Caribbean cruise! Moonlit decks! Soft tropical breezes! While the rest of us plod our weary way through knee-deep snowdrifts." She grinned affectionately at Cherry. "I don't envy you the hot sun though. I freckle and peel like anything."

It had started to snow again so instead of going out they voted to have supper on low tables around the fire. Bertha produced a delicious warmed-over lamb stew. "It always tastes better the second day," she said, ladling out generous portions.

Gwen, complaining good-naturedly, donned over-shoes and went out for vanilla ice cream. Cherry insisted upon making hot fudge sauce to go with it. "Stop treating me like a guest. I'm not a *visiting* nurse. And I know you're all ten times as tired as I am."

But Cherry *was* tired, she discovered an hour later. She fell asleep, as she said afterward, a split second before her head touched the pillow.

She breakfasted with the girls the next morning and shooed them out of the kitchen as she stacked the dishes.

"I'll clean up; you haven't time. The stores won't be open for more than an hour and my appointment with the medical secretary isn't until this afternoon." She added: "I'm kind of excited about that. I believe

I'm going to meet the doctor who'll be my boss on the cruise."

"And he'll be young and handsome, if I know the Ames luck." Gwen chuckled. "Watch out for that tropical moon. You'll come back engaged sure as anything."

Cherry's red cheeks flushed even redder. "Go 'long with you, Jones." She gave Gwen a little push. "He'll probably be ancient and decrepit with a long gray beard. *And* a very nasty disposition."

But Gwen's prediction, not Cherry's, came true. Dr. Kirk Monroe was not only young and handsome, but he had very pleasant manners. Miss Henry, the secretary of the medical department, introduced them in her office after she had given Cherry a sketchy idea of what her duties aboard ship would be like.

"It's all very flexible, Miss Ames." She smiled. "Miss Davis highly recommended you. Said you had an uncanny knack of being able to get along with all sorts of people. That's important."

The compliment made Cherry's dark eyes dance. "I *like* all sorts of people," she admitted.

"Good. Of course," Miss Henry went on, "people do get seasick off Hatteras. And every now and then a member of the crew has an accident. Even more rarely a nurse has to assist at an emergency operation, such as an appendectomy. But, by and large, the people who go on our pleasure cruises are a healthy lot. They go for the fun of it; not because they're invalids or convalescents."

She swiveled around in her chair and pointed out the window. "You can get a glimpse of the *Julita* now. The snowstorm last night delayed her arrival. She docked about an hour ago."

Cherry leaned forward eagerly. Riding in a taxi along the pier-lined North River, she had seen lots of ships. Now she was going to see her own. But, straining her eyes, she saw nothing but two black smokestacks rising above a row of lifeboats. Nevertheless, those smoke-stacks were the chimneys of what was going to be her home-at-sea for twelve whole days!

"It all sounds so wonderful," she told Miss Henry. "I love my work, but I hope everybody stays well. I can't imagine anything more disappointing than getting sick on a pleasure cruise."

"As a matter of fact," the secretary went on, "we did have a really serious case on the *Julita's* last trip. One of those unpredictable, once-in-a-lifetime things. Pulmonary thrombosis. The patient, a man of seventy-odd, died shortly after they took him ashore in Curaçao."

She looked up as the door behind Cherry opened. "Ah, here's Dr. Monroe. He's in charge of sick bay aboard the *Julita*. He'll teach you the ropes after you're aboard ship. Doctor, this is Miss Cherry Ames."

Cherry jumped up and wheeled to face the young man in the doorway. He was as tall and well-built as Charlie, with gray eyes and thick, wavy, brown hair. Cherry thrilled at the sight of his navy-blue uniform with the gold caducei on his sleeves. The second day out, when the weather turned warm, he would change to whites. With his deep coat of even tan, Cherry decided, he would look very handsome in whites.

With sudden embarrassment she realized that she was one of the two principal actors in a little mutual-admiration scene. Dr. Monroe's eyes were dark with approval as he grinned down at her flushed, rosy face.

"He likes my looks, anyway," Cherry thought. She hoped he wouldn't notice how her pulse was racing when they shook hands. "Now, if he only likes *me*, we should make a grand team."

Cherry was glad she had worn her new chocolate-brown suit and the cream-colored blouse that tied in a perky bow under her chin. Melted snow glistened in the dark curls that peeped out from under the brim of her poinsettia-red hat.

Dr. Monroe shook hands warmly. "I'm awfully glad to meet you, Miss Ames." His voice was deep, sincere, and pleasantly husky. His fingers were the clean, strong, cool fingers of a born surgeon.

"I like him already," Cherry admitted frankly to herself. "He's one of those people who are born nice."

Dr. Monroe took two long steps into the office, handed a portfolio of papers to the secretary. "The report on the pulmonary thrombosis case is in there," he said, very sober now. "Hate to lose a patient, but, of course, there was nothing anybody could do. Kind of a nice old fellow. Eccentric, but very co-operative."

Then with a "See you Friday morning" to Cherry he departed.

Cherry, after thanking the secretary for her instructions and advice, left soon afterward. A glance at the nurse's wrist watch that Charlie had given her when she first started on her career told her she still had an hour more before the stores closed.

Cherry finally finished her Christmas shopping late Thursday afternoon. She had the presents gift-wrapped and mailed from the stores with big "Do Not Open Until Xmas" stickers plastered on the brown outside paper. Then she wandered into a novelty shop. She would buy everyone inexpensive little "stocking" gifts too. Yesterday she had bought "jokes" for every member of the Spencer Club. They were all wrapped and hidden on the top shelf of her closet. Her real present to the club was a check toward the new living-room rug. Cherry's check would help make that dream come true.

Buying "stocking" presents in the crowded little shop was fun. She bought one of those new syringelike basters for her mother. Cherry squeezed the rubber bulb and decided it was a giant medicine dropper, but would prove useful when the Christmas turkey was roasting in the oven. For Charlie she chose a trick bow tie equipped with an electric battery. He could make it flash on and off by pressing a button in his pocket. A postage-size deck of Old Maid cards for Midge came next. For Dad she decided on a tiny, wooden bottle labeled "Heart's Desire Perfume." When uncorked, it revealed a miniature mechanical pencil.

It took a long time to find just the right joke for Dr. Joe. Cherry ended up with an inexpensive fountain pen which the manufacturers claimed could be used for underwater writing. She would enclose a note:

"So you can send me an S O S in case you get sealed up in one of your own test tubes."

It was late when she finally left the novelty shop with her bundle of little purchases. Even the impersonal New York crowd was bubbling with pre-Christmas spirit. The snow had turned to slush and here and there were frozen patches which made walking difficult. Every now and then some late Christmas shopper slipped and fell. But the atmosphere was so packed with holiday cheer no one seemed to mind these tumbles.

Lighted Christmas trees were on every block. Wreaths of holly decorated the windows of tall apartment buildings. Cherry wedged herself and her packages through the subway doors and swayed helplessly back and forth with the motion of the train, supported by the other passengers. At last she was wearily sloshing up the steps to No. 9.

The minute Cherry opened the blue door she knew that something was wrong; not wrong exactly, but mysterious. Although no sound came from any one of the rooms, she sensed that she was not alone. She frowned, her hand still on the doorknob. All the lurid tales she had heard about Bohemian Greenwich Village came back.

"Gwen? . . . Josie? . . . Bertha . . . Vivi . . . Mai Lee?"

No answer. For a moment Cherry was almost frightened. Then she shrugged. The inhabitants of Greenwich Village might be informal, but she had always found them very friendly. They were good neighbors, albeit often erratic.

Firmly she closed the door behind her. Then the silence was broken by a giggle. Cherry dropped her packages on the nearest chair. She would know that giggle anywhere. She marched into the living room. Sure enough, crouched behind the sofa was a disheveled-looking Midge Fortune!

Cherry hauled her out and hugged her. "Imp! How in the world did you get here? On a witch's broomstick?"

Midge was so convulsed with laughter she could only point down the hall. Suddenly all three of the bedroom doors opened simultaneously. First Cherry's mother's smiling face popped out; then Dad's, and, last of all, Charlie's towhead.

There were hugs and kisses all around. To add to the confusion the Spencer Club came trooping in en masse.

"We were in on the surprise," Gwen shouted into Cherry's ear above the uproar. "I left my key with the janitor so they could get in."

"But how—why?" Cherry felt as though the calendar had been moved ahead. This must be Christmas Eve; not the eve of her sailing.

It was Charlie who finally explained. "Dad suddenly had to come on business with one of the insurance people. We all felt so depressed after you left us in the lurch, ruining our Christmas plans, we decided to come too."

"We're going to have sort of a Christmas preview here," Josie put in. "This very evening."

"I—I don't understand," Cherry said weakly.

Then Bertha came stolidly down the hall bearing a small but perfectly decorated tree. She plunked it in the middle of the living-room table. Miraculously, before Cherry could blink, presents were heaped up around it—presents of all sizes and shapes in colorful wrappings. And on every tag were the words: "To Cherry."

"We couldn't bear the thought of you spending Christmas on the high seas without any of us," Mrs. Ames was saying.

"You'd get all your presents two weeks late," Mr. Ames added, his eyes twinkling merrily.

Vivian took the floor. "We thought first of mailing them so you'd get them the day after Christmas at Curaçao. But the post office advised us not to. Said anything but air-mail letters would be sure to arrive *after* your ship had gone on to another port. Then they would have to be forwarded back here again."

"Open 'em, honey," Charlie commanded. "And act pleased with mine if it kills you. It can't be exchanged."

Cherry finally came out of her daze. "Give me five minutes, please," she gasped. Scooping up her bundle of "stocking" gifts, she scurried down the hall to her bedroom. She just couldn't open all those presents under the tree without everyone else opening something too.

It took but a few minutes to wrap Christmasy paper around the little last-minute gifts she had bought for her family and Midge, add them to the Spencer Club jokes, and emerge laden with small packages which she dumped helter-skelter around the tree.

"Now," she breathed, "everyone has something. Pitch in. I can't wait."

Cherry opened her mother's present first: a luxurious, white terry-cloth beach robe. Cherry stumbled through the wrappings to hug her mother tightly. "You darling."

Dad's was a cool, sharkskin spectator sports ensemble—slacks, jacket, and blouse—for going ashore. Cherry kissed and scolded him. "You shouldn't have done it. I'll never change back into uniform."

Charlie urged her to open his gift next. "I bought it all by myself," he said. "I'm a nervous wreck for fear it won't fit or you won't like it."

Nestling in folds of white tissue paper was a two-piece American-beauty bathing suit of ruffled taffeta. Just the right size and Cherry's most becoming color. "Charlie," she gasped. "You angel! I'd completely forgotten I'd have to have something glamorous to swim in."

There were ridiculously frivolous but attractive beach clogs from Midge and an enormous, rubber-lined beach bag to match from Dr. Joe. And the Spencer Club had chipped in to buy her the loveliest flowered cotton dancing frock Cherry had ever seen.

It was indeed, as Charlie said, "A very Cherry Christmas!"

They had a festive dinner at one huge table in the exotic Hawaiian Room of the Lexington Hotel. Midge was fascinated when the Honolulu dancers did the hula-hula.

Over dessert of fresh pineapple chunks served in their shells, Cherry outlined the cruise. Charlie lightly marked with his fork an accompanying map of the Caribbean and South America on the tablecloth.

"First stop Curaçao," Cherry told them. "Tuesday morning. And there had better be a big batch of air-mail letters waiting for me."

"There will be." Midge grinned mysteriously. "You'll need a truck."

"Fine." Cherry hurried on. "Next stopover La Guaira, Venezuela. The next day, Puerto Cabello. Then to Cartagena in Colombia. Ditto about air-mail letters at that port. We go straight back to New York from there."

Everybody made careful notes. "I'll check my spelling with an atlas," Gwen promised. "Otherwise expect no word from me."

The Ameses and Midge had engaged rooms at the Lexington. They kissed Cherry good night in the lobby. "See you aboard ship tomorrow."

"I'm going to buy stacks of *leis* and drape them around your neck the way the Hawaiians do," Midge threatened. *"Aloha,"* she finished, proud of the two new words she had added to her vocabulary.

The next minute—or so it seemed to Cherry—it was morning, *the* morning. Since it was a working day, farewells to the Spencer Club were said over breakfast. Cherry had to repack her suitcase to make room for her Christmas presents. Standing in the icy bedroom it was almost impossible to believe that in a day or so the weather aboard ship would be so balmy she could use every one of her gifts.

Then suddenly, weak-kneed and rather shaky, she was climbing up the *Julita's* gangplank. Although the ship would not sail until noon—and it was not yet eleven—several groups of passengers were already aboard. Arm in arm, they trooped along the promenade deck. Others swarmed up the gangplank accompanied by friends who were seeing them off.

Everyone was in a holiday mood. Corsages of exotic orchids were pinned to mink-coated shoulders. Sea gulls circled overhead, mewing catlike. Through the happy shouts and bursts of laughter of the passengers, Cherry heard the intermittent screaming of the winches as the cargo was loaded into the ship's hold. Bang, roll, clank; bang, roll, clank! Cherry had been told that part of the freight would be unloaded at Curaçao. The island had almost no agriculture and imported millions of cases of American canned goods: tomato juice and paste for the hot Spanish dishes; smoked codfish from New England; celery, onions, green peppers, and all kinds of fruit.

Cherry thrilled all over as she took a deep breath of the salty air. It was heavy with the smell of fresh paint, wet steel, water-soaked wood, and creosote.

Hesitantly, she plunked her suitcase down on the deck. Should she try to work her way through the milling crowds and locate her cabin? Or should she wait until a steward or somebody offered help?

A slightly husky voice behind her settled the matter. "Welcome aboard, Miss Ames." It was Dr. Monroe, looking as Midge would have said, "out of this world" in his trim uniform. There was a reassuring grin on his lean, tanned face.

"Good morning," Cherry got out, feeling about as poised as Midge would have felt in similar circumstances. But it was pleasant being on deck with this tall, good-looking man standing protectively beside her.

Then Cherry saw Midge herself galloping up the gangplank with Charlie. Behind them, more sedately, came her father and mother. Cherry proudly introduced her family to Dr. Monroe. Midge was too smitten by the sight of this handsome young man in his glamorous uniform to do anything but stare worshipfully. Time flew. All too soon came the cry "All ashore that's going ashore!"

Last hugs and kisses. *"Bon voyage! Bon voyage!"* Big melting snowflakes pelted their upturned faces as they waved to Cherry from the pier. Tears welled up into her eyes. The gangplank was wheeled away, separating her from her family for Christmas. She couldn't change her mind now.

Someone lightly tapped Cherry's shoulder. "I'm sorry to drag you away, Miss Ames," she heard Dr. Monroe say. "There's been an accident. One of the crew slipped in an oily spot on the engine-room floor. Compound fracture of the right arm."

Dr. Monroe's manner was completely professional now. Cherry sensed that this serious-faced young physician never mixed business with pleasure. She respected him for it. With one last hasty kiss blown from the tip of her fingers straight to her mother, she turned and trotted along the deck after her new boss.

The ship was not yet under way, but she had already started in her new role as Cherry Ames, Cruise Nurse!

CHAPTER III

Sick Bay

AS CHERRY HURRIED TO KEEP UP WITH DR. MONROE'S LONG strides she could feel the pulsating of the ship's engines as the *Julita* got underway. She was glad when the young surgeon stopped long enough to hail a passing steward.

"Waidler," Dr. Monroe said, "this is Miss Ames, the new nurse." He gave the steward Cherry's suitcase. "Take her to her cabin and then show her how to get to sick bay. We have an emergency operation coming up." He turned to Cherry. "I've already ordered the purser, who is also pharmacist's mate, to give the patient one-quarter morphine. I'm on my way to look at the X-ray plates which should be dry by now. As soon as you've changed into uniform go to the operating room and get the emergency tray prepared. Ziegler, the purser, will issue you cap and mask and sterile gown and gloves."

Cherry nodded. His sentences were little clipped commands:

"As soon as you and Ziegler have scrubbed up I want you to prepare the wound. Six washings. Two soapings, two saline, two alcohol, and two Betadine. And of course," he finished with a flicker of a smile on his sober face, "you will chart the patient's T.P.R."

"Yes, doctor." Cherry suddenly felt like a student nurse again for a minute. Would operating aboard ship be so very different that she would forget the routine and be clumsy when she lifted the sterile operating instruments onto the sterile tray? Horrors! She might use the wrong forceps or drop something.

Dr. Monroe strode away with a reassuring nod, and Cherry's courage came back.

The steward, a heavy-browed, stoop-shouldered man, was grumbling: "Come on, miss! I'm a busy man, can't stand here all day while you daydream. I declare, you women's crew are more trouble than the passengers. Seems to me you could carry your own bag. Look healthy enough."

Cherry's red cheeks flamed. "Of course I can carry my own bag, Waidler," she said rather curtly. Then controlling her temper flare-up, she said meekly, "I hate to bother you, but I'm afraid I'd get lost trying to find the way to my cabin and sick bay. And Dr. Monroe wants me there in a hurry."

"Okay, okay," Waidler growled, starting off at a fast trot.

Cherry stumbled after him, depressed by his rudeness. If only she had had an hour or so to get adjusted before being called to assist at an operation! Why did the steward have to be so disagreeable?

She followed him down the long corridor on B deck and noticed that the ship had nothing but outside staterooms. The wide corridor dwindled into a narrow passageway with small cabins on either side. "Women's crew quarters," Waidler said brusquely. He produced a bunch of keys and opened a door leading into a windowless, nine-by-twelve room.

"Why, there's not even a porthole," Cherry thought, momentarily disappointed. "I'll suffocate." Then she remembered that the *Julita* was air-conditioned. The cabin, though tiny, was attractively furnished. There was a bright-flowered chintz spread on the comfortable-looking maple bed, with a matching slip cover on the big easy chair. On one side of the room was a small maple desk with a straight-back chair; on the other, she saw a dressing table and a mirrored door opening into a small but compact closet.

Cherry had time for only a brief glimpse of her cabin. Waidler set down her suitcase just inside the door, handed her a key, and started off again.

"First I'll show you Doc's suite," he muttered gruffly. "Bedroom, office, and the dispensary. Your office opens into it. On the starboard side, after section of B deck. Sick bay is right below. Starboard side, after section, C deck," he finished in the supercilious tone of one speaking to a very stupid child. "Do you think you can find your way around now?"

Cherry's mind reeled, but she said with forced cheerfulness, "Oh, yes, thank you very much, Waidler."

"Don't thank me," Waidler retorted sourly. "That's what I get paid for. Although some people think they cause me enough trouble so it's worth a dime tip anyway."

Cherry went icy cold with embarrassment and inner confusion. She had taken it for granted that since they were both employees he would have been insulted if she had offered a tip. After all, that type of thing worked both ways. If he became ill, she would nurse him faithfully without expecting a gratuity. That was her job, just as the few begrudged minutes he had spent with her were his.

She fumbled in her change purse and produced a quarter. He accepted it expressionlessly and left her outside the doctor's suite without a word.

Cherry hurried back down the corridor to her cabin. Hastily, she changed into uniform, white stockings, and rubber-soled white shoes.

"Oh, dear," she thought, locking the door behind her, "I hope the other employees aren't going to be as uncooperative as Waidler."

Then, remembering her first pleasant impression of the young ship's surgeon, she cheered up. The important thing was that she and Dr. Monroe should make a good team. According to what Miss Henry had told her in the medical offices on the pier, she would have very little to do with the rest of the crew. And none of the passengers would even know of her existence unless one of them became ill.

And then, hurrying along the corridor, she banged right into one of the passengers. A stateroom door was suddenly thrust open and out popped a slim young girl, right in Cherry's path. They collided for one breathless moment, and then both of them laughed, apologizing:

"I'm sorry. I wasn't looking where I was going."

"It was my fault," Cherry insisted tactfully. "I'm in a frightful hurry to help with an operation."

The girl, who looked about sixteen or seventeen, had thick golden-blond braids wound around her head. Cherry noted briefly that her huge hazel eyes showed signs of recent weeping. The reddened eyes grew even wider with respect and awe as she stared at Cherry's crisply starched uniform.

"Oh, you're the ship's nurse," she breathed. "How wonderful! It must be marvelous to have a career."

"It is wonderful." Cherry smiled. "I love my profession."

"My name's Jan," the tall, slim girl blurted out. "Jan Paulding. I want to be an artist, but my mother—"

A querulous voice from inside the stateroom interrupted: "Jan. *Jan!* Please close that door. I feel a draft."

Cherry gave Jan a friendly wave and hurried down the linoleum-covered stairs to C deck. She found sick bay without any trouble at all. It contained two wards, one for men and one for women, with upper and lower bunks in each ward.

"Why, it's a miniature hospital," Cherry thought with an approving glance at the white-tiled walls, the spotless sink, the gleaming instruments that lined the walls of the tiny instrument room. In the center of the operating room, lying on a long table under a powerful lamp, was the patient, his face white under a spattering of freckles. He looked like a drowsy-eyed boy and he smiled cheerfully up at Cherry as she checked his temperature, pulse, and respiration. The purser, who Cherry guessed would act as "scrub nurse" during the emergency operation, was already in coveralls, cap, mask, and gloves.

With a friendly nod he introduced himself as "Ziggy." Before she began to scrub, Ziegler handed her a cap and mask. Cherry carefully adjusted the strings on the cap so that the flap completely covered her dark curls. Then she turned to the sink as she pulled the mask up over her mouth and nose. She waited while Ziggy adjusted the little hourglass above the sink. "When all the sand shifts from the top to the bottom," he told her, "you'll know you've scrubbed for at least twelve minutes."

Halfway through, the ship rolled, and Cherry, who had not yet got her sea legs, lost her balance for a second. One of her fingers brushed against the side of the sink.

With a shrug, Ziegler adjusted the hourglass again. "Don't mind that, Miss Cherry," he said kindly. "We all make slips."

Cherry, as she started to scrub all over again, decided that there *was* a difference between operating on a deck and operating on a nice, steady floor!

And it was very generous of a seasoned sailor like the purser not to have lost patience with a landlubber nurse.

Once scrubbed, Ziggy helped her into a sterile gown and gloves, being careful not to contaminate them. Ziegler then unpinned the big surgical bundle. Deftly avoiding contact with the inside of the bundle, he turned it upside down and dumped the sterile contents on the sterile O.R. tray.

Using the big forceps that always reminded Cherry of ice tongs, she set up the O.R. equipment: Sheets, towels, swabs, gauze bandages, vaseline, solutions— she did not yet even touch her gloved hands to the can of sterile powder with which she would later dust the interior of the surgeon's gloves.

As she worked, Ziegler said, "Bill, that's the patient, has already had his Ether. He'll be asleep in a minute."

Cherry knew about Ether, the wonderful anesthetic. But she wondered about the purser who seemed to know almost as much as an intern. She asked him point-blank:

"What are you anyway, Mr. Ziegler? A combination purser and pharmacist's mate?"

He grinned. "Call me Ziggy, Miss Cherry. Everybody does. I've been with this line since I was a kid like Bill. And I'm ex-Merchant Marine. Went to the pharmacist's mate school during the war. Had eighteen months of what you R.N.'s would probably call nothing but elementary first aid training. I've had lots of practice since school, though. Assisted at all sorts of emergency operations at sea." He chuckled reminiscently. "Most of the time there wasn't anybody else *but* me to help the surgeon. You pick up a lot of know-how when you have to."

"You certainly do," Cherry agreed, remembering her own experiences as an Army nurse. She liked this ex-merchant seaman. He was small and compactly built, with an ageless but battered face which made her guess that he might well have been a boxer at one time or another.

Now to prepare the wound.

Bill was completely anesthetized and Cherry had just finished the eighth washing when Dr. Monroe came into the operating room. He slipped on his cap and mask, and as he scrubbed up said succinctly:

"X ray showed a compound fracture of the humerus, noncomminuted, not impacted." Dr. Monroe added: "If it had happened a few minutes earlier we would have put the boy ashore."

Cherry knew that the complicated-sounding medical phrases simply meant that the operation would be *un*-complicated. The surgeon would not have to probe for fragments of broken bone in the upper part of Bill's arm. The bone would be set and the wound sutured with very little risk of infection.

Cherry was glad of that. Bill would, of course, wear a cast for many weeks, but he looked like the kind of a boy who would manage very well with his right arm in a sling.

She draped the patient in sterile sheets and arranged sterile towels around the wound. Dr. Monroe held out his arms. Cherry helped him into his gown and slipped rubber gloves on his hands. Ziggy, standing behind the surgeon, tied the strings that held his gown in place.

It was routine after that: the debridement—cutting away dead tissue, reducing the fracture, and suturing the wound. Cherry's hands were steady and she anticipated every one of Dr. Monroe's quiet, staccato orders:

"Scalpel . . . forceps . . . sponge . . . suture . . . penicillin and sulfa solution . . . vaseline gauze . . ."

At last it was over and Bill's arm was in a cast.

Cherry took a deep breath of the warm, soapy, sweet air in the tiny room. Had she made good? Did Dr. Monroe now feel as she did that they were a good team?

His gray eyes smiled at her above the mask. "Thanks, Miss Ames. It's a pleasure to work with someone who really is efficient."

Then he was gone. A minute or so later a redheaded young man in a short, white coat came into sick bay. "Rick, the emergency orderly, reporting, ma'am." He grinned at Cherry. "Doc says I'm to sit with Bill for the rest of the day."

Cherry hastily rubbed away the frown that creased her forehead and forced her lips into a smile of greeting. But she didn't like it at all. Was she to leave the patient, stiil under anesthesia, to the care of a mere boy?

"Take over, Rick, from here on in," Ziggy said. "Miss Cherry and I have work to do. But first help me get the patient into bed."

Cherry watched them worriedly, but relaxed as she saw that they lifted Bill from the operating table with efficient gentleness, and. settled him comfortably in a lower bunk. Cherry took the patient's pulse and saw that he was breathing normally. Rick drew up a chair to the side of the bunk and sat down. Unconcernedly, he produced a comic book from an inside pocket of his jacket.

"Don't worry about me and Bill, Miss Cherry," he said. "We're buddies. If he gets to thrashing around I'll read to him. Or conk him over the head," he finished with a mischievous grin.

So Cherry left them together, reluctantly, because they both seemed so very young. Together she and Ziggy cleaned up O.R., the purser chatting conversationally all the while.

"Nice guy, Doc. Never loses his temper when a guy makes a mistake. Dropped a thermometer last trip and he didn't say a word. Guess he was almost as nervous as I was. We all knew we were going to lose that pulmonary thrombosis case. What can you do when a guy gets a blood clot in his lungs? And we had to think of the other passengers. A death on a pleasure cruise isn't what they paid out their money for. Doc and I didn't think the old fellow would last until we docked at Willemstad. But he did. Had an iron constitution, I guess, for all that he must have been way past seventy."

Cherry worked swiftly and deftly, listening with only half of her mind. She hoped they wouldn't have another tragic case this trip. But lightning didn't strike twice at the same place. Or did it?

"Like all physicians, Dr. Monroe hates to lose a case," she said to Ziggy. "What was the old gentleman like?"

"My guess," the purser said as he wheeled away the instrument table and tray, "is that he had spent a lot of time at sea, during his youth, and not too long ago either. Had that weather-beaten, seafaring look. A rough diamond but a nice character, although peculiar. Doc and I liked him, but Waidler, the steward assigned to his cabin, couldn't get on with him at all."

Laughter bubbled up to Cherry's red lips. "You'd have to be a saint to get along with Waidler, I imagine."

"That you would," the purser agreed emphatically. "Personally, it's all I can do to keep a civil tongue in my head when he's in one of his moods. But for all his fits of bad temper, he's a good employee and has been with the line as long as I have. Knows the ropes better than any other member of the crew. Efficient as all get out. But even *he* slips up every now and then. Like at Willemstad last trip—" Ziggy suddenly clamped his mouth shut.

Cherry wondered what the rest of the sentence might have been. In what way had the efficient Waidler slipped up? Mildly curious, she would have enjoyed hearing how the disagreeable steward had got himself into some sort of scrape. But Ziggy adroitly changed the subject.

"Oh, jimminy, I forgot." He handed her two sheets of typewritten pages. "Doc told me to give you this first thing."

The pages were headed: "Duties of a Ship Nurse."

Cherry scanned them hurriedly, then decided to read the instructions carefully back in her own cabin.

"It's a lot of hokum," Ziggy said gruffly. "No swimming-pool privileges for either you or Doc. What's the matter with the powers that be? One would think you two, the cleanest people aboard ship, might contaminate the water. Naturally the crew doesn't expect, or *want*, to mingle with the passengers any more than they have to. But you and Doc are professional people. Passengers ought to consider themselves lucky if you gave 'em a little of your spare time."

Cherry gulped, thinking of Charlie's Christmas present. But she wasn't going to be able to wear that lovely American-beauty suit in the glamorous outdoor, tiled pool after all.

Then she laughed and said, "There'll be plenty of time for swimming when we're in port."

"Not so much," Ziggy told her. "Look at Rule Four." He pointed a stubby finger at the first page of her instructions, quoting by heart:

"When in port the ship's nurse is never to go ashore without first obtaining permission from the ship's surgeon. The nurse and ship's surgeon may not have shore leave at the same time."

Cherry couldn't help giggling. It sounded like old times.

"Well," Ziggy said with relief, "I'm glad you don't seem to mind the red tape too much. But maybe you won't feel like laughing when you read Rule Five."

Cherry read it swiftly. "In foreign ports the nurse is to report aboard ship and in uniform to the surgeon at least one full hour before the scheduled sailing time."

She refused to allow these restrictions to depress her. "Dr. Monroe's just naturally nice," she told Ziggy. "And I know he'll he more than fair. He'll give me plenty of shore leave. After all, you can only do just so much sight-seeing. And I can't do a lot of shopping. I've already spent most of my money on Christmas presents."

"You're a good sport," Ziggy said approvingly. "Come on. I'll show you the dispensary on B deck. Then we'll go up to my office on A deck. We keep the medical refrigerator in there. You'll want to be able to locate quickly, the penicillin and other drugs that deteriorate unless kept on ice. You'll also need ice cubes for ice bags once in a while."

After a quick inventory of the dispensary, Cherry was satisfied that the ship was adequately supplied with medication, gauze, bandages, etc. Then Ziggy escorted her to the purser's office.

He unlocked the door and then sucked in his breath sharply as he moved inside. "The safe!" Cherry heard him say. "It's been broken into."

Cherry peered around his broad back. The door of the little safe gaped open, and the floor around it was littered with papers and legal-looking envelopes!

Ziggy was already down on his hands and knees, checking the rifled contents of the safe's drawers. Cherry stood uncertainly watching him. Should she quietly go away or offer to help?

"Somebody awfully smart pulled this job," Ziggy muttered. "Somebody who knew I'd be down in sick bay for more than an hour, safely out of his way. Somebody who knows how to pick locks; somebody mighty familiar with safe combinations. Somebody smart enough to guess we always set this combination to correspond with our sailing dates. This one," he explained in an undertone, more to himself than to Cherry, "was set for one-o-two-o-two-two: the twenty-second day of the twelfth month, you see."

Cherry couldn't help reflecting that Waidler might well know that the safe combination was set to correspond with the ship's sailing date. He had also heard Dr. Monroe order Cherry to sick bay for an emergency operation. And the disagreeable steward could have counted on the purser being called on to assist as the pharmacist's mate.

Hastily Cherry quieted her suspicions. It wasn't fair to suspect Waidler simply because he had been rude to her. Dozens of passengers and other stewards might have overheard Dr. Monroe telling Cherry of the accident. Any member of the crew would have known the purser would be out of his office then, too. A passenger familiar with shipboard procedure would have known the purser would be called on to assist at the operation.

Ziggy suddenly straightened up. He turned around to Cherry, the expression on his face one of complete bafflement.

"Well, I'll be tied to the mast before the skipper!" he exploded. "Not a single, solitary thing has been taken. And let me tell you, Miss Cherry, there's enough jewelry in that drawer alone to buy and sell this ship!"

~~~~~~

CHAPTER IV

Timmy

ZIGGY, STILL MUTTERING TO HIMSELF IN BEWILDERMENT, replaced the contents of the safe. "I don't get it, Miss Cherry," he kept saying. "Who would want to go to all the trouble of breaking into the safe and then go off without taking even a gold-plated pin?"

He reset the dial with a new combination and handed Cherry a duplicate key to his office. He also gave her a key to the outside door of the dispensary and another one for her own office.

"I've got to go and report to the master," he said. "But you might take a look through the refrigerator while I'm gone. If you need anything like canned juices you want kept chilled, Waidler will get 'em for you."

He hurried away. Cherry checked the contents of the refrigerator, saw that it was well stocked and that all the ice trays were filled.

Then carefully locking the door behind her, she went down to her cabin, wondering who had broken into the safe. And why. Before unpacking her bag, she carefully read her instructions. Cherry noticed with relief that in general the duties of a ship's nurse were very similar to those of a nurse connected with a hospital, a clinic, or a doctor's office.

In a hospital nurses ate at stated times. If they were late to meals, they went without. On board ship she was to eat half an hour before the passengers.

In a hospital nurses were not allowed to eat in the wards. On a ship, apparently, the nurse did not eat in the big dining room that ran amidships completely through from port to starboard. She would eat in the small, staff grill. But that was where Dr. Monroe would have his meals too.

Cherry couldn't help hoping that one of her "duties" would be sitting at the same table with the ship's surgeon. As though in answer to her question, someone tapped on the door. It was Dr. Kirk Monroe.

"Aren't you starving?" he asked. "We missed lunch, but I ordered a snack sent up to the grill. It's waiting for us now. Soup and sandwiches and cake." He smiled at her trim, uniformed figure. "You don't look as though you had to diet."

Cherry grinned, pleased at the implied compliment. "It's a good thing I don't. I'm ravenous practically all the time."

They strolled up two flights of stairs to the promenade deck. Cherry discovered with pleasure that the staff dining room was a cozy little grill, decorated informally but attractively with a red-and-gold color scheme.

"Sometimes passengers eat in here," Dr. Monroe said. "Mostly children with their mothers or nurses. That's why we have to show up half an hour ahead of time."

Cherry had not realized how hungry she was until she tasted the delicious cream of asparagus soup. The chicken sandwiches were delicious too.

"When you finish your second piece of cake," Dr. Monroe said, grinning, "I'll take you on a sightseeing tour of the ship."

"But what about our patient?" Cherry asked. "I didn't like leaving him alone with that boy while he was still anesthetized. But," she finished, her eyes twinkling as she quoted Rule 9 word for word:

"When in doubt the ship's nurse is always to be guided by the ship's surgeon. She receives her orders directly from him, and must never assume any responsibility except at his direction."

The young physician laughed. "That's right, Miss Cherry Ames. I'm your boss. And Rick is completely trustworthy. He's had some orderly experience in different hospitals in New York and during the war he was a corpsman with the Marines."

"I know," Cherry said, "but still—"

"Relax, Nurse," Dr. Monroe interrupted, pretending to be stern. "I looked in on Bill before I came to invite you to lunch. He's conscious and quite comfortable, reading a comic book, believe it or not. The bell beside his bunk rings in the purser's office, as well as in yours and mine. Ziggy and Rick will take turns keeping an eye on him from now on. Except for routine checks of his temperature, pulse, and respiration, you can pretty much dismiss that patient from your mind. We'll run into seasickness tonight as we approach Hatteras. There's a storm brewing and if the seas are very rough you may not get much sleep. As a precaution, I'd like you to take a nap this afternoon and rest and relax as much as possible in-between times. A tired nurse is apt to be cranky, and one of the best cures for seasickness is a calm, cheerful attitude."

Cherry nodded. "Outside of being calm and cheerful, what do I do for seasick passengers?"

For answer Dr. Monroe reached into his pocket and produced a small package bearing the label of a well-known pharmaceutical house. He dumped two tiny pieces of chewing gum on the tablecloth. "These contain mostly atropine to relieve the spasms and phenobarbital to quiet the nerves." He pushed back his chair and stood up. "Let's go and tour the ship."

The grill where the staff was served meals was right off the main dining room on the promenade deck. Cherry stared in wonder at the tall columns and wide casement windows.

"That dome," Dr. Monroe said, pointing to the high ceiling, "rolls back, opening to the sky. All very *al fresco.*"

"And glamorous," Cherry said, awed.

They wandered aft to the little night club that opened onto the veranda above the beach deck and the pool. Cherry saw that the colorful murals on the walls were scenes of foreign places they would visit en route. An orchestra was tuning up for tea dancing on the highly polished floor.

Out on the breeze-swept veranda they looked down at the blue-tiled pool. "Tomorrow night," Dr. Monroe said, "it'll be good and warm. Then they'll turn on this flood-light and the underwater lights. A lot of the passengers spend most of their time in and around the pool."

"I don't blame them," Cherry sighed. "I understand it's off bounds for us."

"It certainly is," Dr. Monroe told her with mock severity. "And don't ever let me catch you out of uniform except when you're on shore leave. The Old Man's very strict about all the proprieties. He has an attack of apoplexy at the slightest breach of shipboard etiquette. But," he finished with a twinkle in his long gray eyes, "I imagine your experience as an Army nurse will make it easy for you to conform."

Cherry told him then about some of her experiences. It turned out that they had both been stationed in the Pacific at the same time, but with different units. It was fun to talk shop with another veteran as they absorbed the quiet, restful charm of the paneled library, the cool informality of the pleasant lounges, the spacious beauty of the Georgian living room. This salon, which ran forward from port to starboard, had tall French windows that led to a palm-flanked solarium.

While they were standing there, a petty officer came up to them. "Passenger calling for you, Doctor," he said. "Mrs. Crane, Suite 141-143, B deck. Her little boy came aboard with a cold. She thinks he may be running a fever."

"There goes my nap," Cherry thought. Colds at this time of the year were not to be treated lightly. They were often forerunners of influenza, laryngitis, croup, and even pneumonia.

The young surgeon's manner was so professional now that he might just as well have been wearing his white hospital coat. "No need for you to accompany me, Nurse," he told Cherry, striding across the living room. "I'll send for you if I need your help."

"But I'd like to come, Doctor," she said, trotting along beside him. "I'm pretty good with sick little boys, if I do say so myself."

They were out in the corridor now and whatever the ship's surgeon's reply might have been was drowned in the loud-speaker's blare:

"Calling Dr. Monroe . . . Dr. Mon—roe. Calling Dr. Monroe . . ."

So Cherry went along anyway. In a few minutes a small, fragile-looking woman was admitting them to the luxurious living room of Suite 141-143.

"Oh, Doctor," she said worriedly, "I'm so glad you came right away. Timmy's been coughing quite a lot for the past few days, but otherwise he seemed to be completely over his cold. But now he sounds so hoarse and looks so feverish." She led them into the adjoining bedroom. "He got away from me for a few minutes after lunch. I found him out on that windy veranda above the pool."

Cherry's heart went out to the curly-haired little boy who was propped up against pillows in one of the twin beds. His face was flushed and his eyes were slightly glazed, indicating an above-normal temperature.

Dr. Monroe smiled down at him reassuringly before making an examination. "Hello, Timmy. I'm Dr. Monroe and this nice nurse is Miss Cherry Ames."

Timmy's round face puckered into a grin. "Cherry!" he hooted in a hoarse voice. "That's not a girl's name. A cherry is something you eat with pits in it. I swallowed a pit once," he said proudly. "And I didn't even have a tummy-ache. I've swallowed lots of orange pits," he went on, boasting. "But Mummy doesn't know that I swallowed a great big cherry pit once."

Dr. Monroe laughed. "When I was a little boy I swallowed an olive seed. My mother said if I ever did it again olive branches would grow right out of my mouth."

"Mothers are fussy, aren't they?" Timmy said in very man-to-man aside.

The young surgeon cocked an eyebrow quizzically. "But kind of nice, too, aren't they, Timmy?"

Timmy wriggled in mischievous glee, knowing perfectly well his mother could hear every word of the conversation. "We-ell," he admitted with pretended reluctance, "that 'pends. It 'pends on how many chapters they read when they put you to bed. It 'pends on how many times they make you wash your hands."

While they were talking, Dr. Monroe was opening the kit he had picked up on his way to the suite. "That reminds me," he told Timmy. "Miss Ames and I have to wash our hands too. May we use your bathroom?"

"Sure," Timmy said with a magnanimous wave of his pudgy little hand. It was obviously beyond him why anybody would want to wash unless ordered to by his mother.

After they had scrubbed, Dr. Monroe shook down his sterile thermometer. "How old are you, Timmy?" he asked in his quiet, friendly voice. "Eight? Nine?"

Timmy howled with laughter. "Naw. I'm six. And I'm in the second grade and I can read and write and sometimes I get the right answers in 'rithmetic."

Mrs. Crane hovered nearer. "Stop talking, Timmy. It just makes your throat worse."

Cherry bit her lip. She knew Dr. Monroe was encouraging Timmy to relax while he was taking the rectal temperature and she took the little boy's pulse and respiration. Was pretty, young Mrs. Crane going to be one of those interfering mothers?

Dr. Monroe glanced at the thermometer and then handed it to Cherry. The mercury had stopped at 101°. Nothing much for a six-year-old but an indication of an infection that should be checked. Now Dr. Monroe was listening to Timmy's heart and lungs. "Breathe deeply, Timmy," he said. "In and out, in and out, that's fine."

The little boy was seized with a coughing spasm. Dr. Monroe bent his head lower, frowning in concentration. Then he turned Timmy on his stomach and began thumping his back. At last he raised his head and hung his stethoscope around his neck. He examined the child carefully from head to foot and stood up to speak to Mrs. Crane.

Cherry helped Timmy slip back into his pajamas and listened. "There's nothing for you to worry about, Mrs. Crane, but we don't want him to go into croup. So we'll keep him warm and quiet, and Miss Ames will give him half an aspirin and an inhalation every four hours. She will also take his temperature at that time. It may well go up this evening, but don't be alarmed. If it seems indicated, we'll start him at once on sulfa."

He turned to Cherry. "You will, of course, force fluids and keep this young man quiet." He repacked his bag and started for the door. "Perhaps, Miss Ames, it would be advisable for you to instruct Mrs. Crane in the care of the patient. You may be needed elsewhere tonight and I do not wish his treatment interrupted."

When he had gone, Mrs. Crane looked at Cherry with frightened eyes. "Oh, dear," she moaned, "I'm helpless with sick people. I don't even know how to read a thermometer. Timmy has a nurse, you see, but I didn't think I'd need her on such a short cruise. I thought it would be fun to have Timmy all to myself."

She sank down on the foot of the boy's bed and Cherry saw with amazement that she was actually trembling. How could she teach this panicky little woman how to care for her child? Patiently, Cherry began with the thermometer which she would have to sterilize before returning it to the doctor's kit. But she met with little success.

Mrs. Crane could barely read the numbers and she could not see the mercury at all. Timmy thought it was all very funny and insisted upon being shown the silver line himself. To his mother's chagrin, he located it at once.

"It's stopped at 101," he chortled smugly.

Cherry shook it down to 96°. Timmy found it again without too much difficulty. Mrs. Crane tried again but without much hope. She twirled the glass instrument over and over in her slim, beringed fingers.

"It's no use," she said after a moment. "I'm just one of those people who can't read thermometers."

Cherry gave up. She hurried to the dispensary for aspirin and the inhalation equipment. Back in the bedroom she plugged in the electric vaporizer. "You fill the jar about two-thirds full of water," she told Mrs. Crane, "to allow for bubbling over. Add a scant pinch of salt. That makes the water boil more quickly. The medication, a teaspoon of tincture of benzoin, goes in this little trap under the lid. Simple, isn't it?"

Mrs. Crane moaned. "I didn't take in a word you said."

Cherry sighed inwardly but kept her face placid with her most professional smile. "Now we'll make a tent. Have you an umbrella?"

Mrs. Crane produced one from the closet, pathetically pleased to find there was one task she could perform.

As Cherry opened the dainty white silk umbrella, Timmy let out a yell. "That's bad luck. Close it up quickly, Cherry. Opening a 'brella indoors is worse luck than walking under a ladder."

"Don't be silly, Timmy," Mrs. Crane said. "And don't call the nurse Cherry. Her name is Miss Ames."

Cherry laughed. "I like to be called Cherry by nice young patients." She added to Timmy: "The only bad luck you can get by walking under a ladder is if it happens to fall on you. That's why it's smart to walk around them. And as for an umbrella, you just have to be careful not to poke anybody in the eye. Here, you hold the handle and keep it steady for me."

Timmy looked up at her round-eyed, but he had a firm grip on the curved handle. "What are you going to do to me now?" he demanded suspiciously.

"I'm going to cover you all up in a tent," Cherry said, shaking the folds out of a clean sheet. "I'm going to drape this over your umbrella, and you've got to help by telling me when you're tucked inside your tent as snug as a bug in a rug."

Timmy giggled, no longer suspicious. "I'll pe-tend I'm the Talking Cricket," he said. "Like the one in *Pinocchio.*"

Steam, fragrant with the aroma of resin, was pouring from the spout of the vaporizer. Cherry set it on a low table beside Timmy's head. Then she draped the sheet over the umbrella.

"All covered, Timmy? Not a tiny breath of the delicious steam must be allowed to get out of your tent."

"All covered," came his muffled reply.

"Don't touch the vaporizer," Cherry cautioned. "It's as hot as anything. Just lie back as quietly as you can and breathe in and out, in and out."

"Okay," Timmy agreed, "but you've got to read to me. I can't keep still less somebody reads to me."

Cherry glanced at her wrist watch. In a few minutes it would be four o'clock, time for her to go down to sick bay and take Bill's T.P.R. Surely she could leave the little boy alone with his mother for a few minutes.

Mrs. Crane, reading Cherry's thoughts, picked up a bright-jacketed book. "I'll read, Timmy," she offered. "Miss Cherry is too busy. She has other patients, you know."

A threatening silence from the other side of the sheet told Cherry this proposal was not being met with enthusiasm. Finally he said in a fretful voice:

"Oh, all *right*. But you come right back, Cherry, or I'll punch a hole in this tent."

Cherry, laughing, whispered to Mrs. Crane, "I won't be gone more than a few minutes." Timmy's mother looked as though she were sure the vaporizer was going to explode any second and blow Timmy, tent and all, right up to the boat deck.

Then Cherry, moving silently on her rubber-soled shoes, tiptoed across the thick bedroom carpet to the door leading to the main corridor. Quietly she turned the knob and slipped out. On the other side of the door she again collided with tall, young Jan Paulding!

The slim girl shrank back and seemed to be completely at a loss for words.

"This is getting to be a habit," Cherry gasped. But deep down inside her she couldn't help wondering: "Why was she standing just outside Timmy's bedroom? Because that's what she must have been doing! But *why*? Eavesdropping? Ridiculous! Nothing of interest except to the parties concerned has been said for the past half-hour."

Cherry started down the corridor thinking, "What interest could a young society subdeb possibly have in Stateroom 141?" She muttered to herself, "Keep your apron on, Ames. Just because you've nose-dived into some mysteries before is no reason there has to be one on a vacation cruise!"

CHAPTER V

Mr. Rough Diamond

FOR SOME REASON, CHERRY TURNED AROUND HALFWAY down the corridor. She came back to the obviously still embarrassed young girl.

"Forgive me, Jan," she said, "I didn't mean to be so abrupt. Have you a little magnet in your pocket that makes me keep on running smack into you every time we meet?"

Jan, unsmiling, backed away tautly. Her slim fingers went up to her thick, coiled braids. "I—I'm s-sorry," she stuttered. "I b-beg your p-pardon."

Cherry grinned. "It was as much my fault as yours. I sneaked out of that room purposely, but not for the purpose of knocking the breath out of you. I've a fretful little patient in there. A six-year-old boy who will very probably go into croup sometime this evening."

"Oh?" Jan's pale eyebrows shot up into little inverted V's of interest. "A little boy? Sick?"

"That's right." Cherry started to move away again.

"How sick?" Jan's voice was very tense. You might have thought the little boy was her own brother. "Croup? Does that mean he'll be wakeful at night?"

"No, indeed," Cherry said, a trifle impatiently, wishing she hadn't mentioned Timmy at all. It had been a mild violation of professional ethics—discussing her little patient with an outsider. And now as punishment she had got herself involved in a conversation that would delay her all along the line. *Here I go again,* she thought ruefully: *The late Miss Ames!* Aloud she said crisply, "Sorry to be rude, but I must run along. See you again."

She could feel Jan's hazel eyes following her all the way down the corridor until she turned into the narrow passageway that ended in the stairs leading down to C deck. Someone was coming up the stairs with a tray of tea and little cakes. Cherry saw that it was her unfriendly steward.

"Oh, Waidler," she said, trying hard to sound cordial and professional at once, "I'm glad to have run into you. Would you please bring a large glass of pineapple juice and a small dish of applesauce to 141? I've a sick little boy in there."

Waidler glowered at her. "Since when do I start taking orders from you? Get that stuff yourself. This is teatime. Trays. Trays. Trays. Pineapple juice and applesauce, my eye!"

He started up the steps past her. Cherry caught her lower lip between her teeth and mentally counted ten.

"I'm sorry," she said firmly, "but I'm afraid I'll have to insist. Just this once. I have two patients in need of attention at the same time. Dr. Monroe ordered fluids and aspirin for the little Crane boy. I need the apple-sauce to disguise the bitter taste of the aspirin."

Two red spots appeared on Waidler's prominent cheekbones. He hesitated.

Cherry said quickly: "On your next trip to B deck from the galley you can easily add my order to a tea tray. I'm sorry I seem to be a nuisance, but it won't happen again. At my first free moment I shall give you a list of items, such as juices and fruit, which I shall wish to keep in the refrigerator in the purser's office. I shall also want some bouillon cubes, a jar of instant coffee, a pot of jam, and some packaged Melba toast. Once my shelves are stocked I shall not need to trouble you again."

Waidler's heavy brows were knitted into a dark frown. "You don't want much, do you?" he sneered. He went on up the stairs grumbling, "Make out a requisition and I'll see what I can do. Purser's got to sign the requisition. I ain't going to get into trouble for any red-faced bossy little nurse."

But Cherry knew that he had been impressed with her list of requirements. She could make tea, coffee, and broth henceforth on the little electric grill she had discovered in the dispensary. It would mean less work for Waidler in the end.

Down in sick bay she found Bill complaining that he wanted to get up. "I feel fine, Miss Cherry," he insisted when she found that his temperature was normal.

"What's a broken arm? I got a bullet in my shoulder during the war and went right on working."

'That was different," Cherry said, glad to note that his color was good, his pulse normal. "You *had* to go on working then. Now you must keep warm and quiet to avoid shock and to prevent infection of the wound."

Rick chuckled. "He's as stubborn as a mule, Miss Cherry. But don't you give him another thought. Purser told me where he keeps the strait jacket."

"Strait jacket?" Bill howled. He doubled up his left fist. "Just you try it, brother. With my right arm in a cast I can still knock you from here to Curaçao without even—"

"Sh, sh," Cherry commanded. "You do as Rick says or I'll fix you up in a restraining bed."

Bill grinned. "Okay, Miss Cherry. I'll be good."

Cherry, consulting her bedside notes, charted both Bill's and Timmy's T.P.R. in the sick-bay log. Then she hurried back up to the Crane suite. There she found everything in confusion.

Mrs. Crane had somehow tripped on the electric cord and knocked over the vaporizer. Fortunately it had fallen to the floor, not on Timmy. But Mrs. Crane was sucking a burnt finger tip and Timmy was playing parachutist with the umbrella. Cherry snatched away the remnants of her tent and tucked the little boy firmly back in bed.

She hurried into the bathroom and made a paste of bicarbonate of soda and water. "Keep your finger tip in this for a while," she told Mrs. Crane. "I'll bandage it with Chloresium ointment later."

"What's zat?" Timmy demanded curiously. "Sounds awful. Does it hurt?"

As Cherry repaired the damage to the rug and the floor and started the vaporizer again, she explained:

"It's a marvelous new salve which we use for cuts and burns and lots of other things. It works almost like magic because it's made from chlorophyll."

"What's so wonderful about that?" Timmy said doubtfully. "*I* never even heard of it."

"Chlorophyll," Cherry said patiently, "is what makes plants green. The ointment looks black when it comes out of the tube, but when I spread it on your mummy's finger you'll see how green it is."

"Do it now. *Now!* I wanna see that klor-klor-whatever it is." Timmy began to bounce up and down. "Is it really magic, Cherry? Honest and truly cross-your-heart magic, Cherry?"

Cherry shook her head. "No, not quite, but after I put it on, your mummy's finger won't hurt any more. And she may not even have a blister."

"Get that green stuff," Timmy ordered. "I don't want my mummy's finger to hurt!"

Cherry realized that Timmy was not going to relax until he had seen his mother's finger bandaged. "Whatever I do, I always seem to make matters worse," she groaned inwardly. "If Dr. Kirk Monroe comes in now and finds that Timmy hasn't had either his aspirin or inhalation he won't think I'm efficient any more."

Thankful that the doctor's suite adjoined the Cranes', she hurried next door to the dispensary for a tube of

Chloresium ointment and a package of Band-Aids. When she came back, the pineapple juice and dish of applesauce had arrived. Steam was pouring from the vaporizer's spout by the time she had bandaged Mrs. Crane's finger. But Cherry decided Timmy must have his medication before the inhalation.

She crushed half an aspirin tablet into a powder and mixed it with a little of the applesauce. She smiled at Timmy. "Open your mouth and shut your eyes."

The little boy promptly reversed the order.

"Timmy!" Mrs. Crane said sharply. "Don't you want to get well and go swimming in that beautiful pool?"

Timmy, teeth clamped together, shook his dark curls.

"But you don't want to miss fire drill," Cherry said. "That's fun. You have to strap on that life preserver on the wall over there and hurry out on deck to find your lifeboat."

Timmy gobbled up the applesauce in two gulps. At last he was tucked under the tent. Cherry decided to remain in the room for the duration of the steaming. Heaven knows what might happen if she left Mrs. Crane in charge.

When the inhalation was over, Cherry told Timmy: "I'll pop in to see you at bedtime. Around eight. Now keep nice and quiet and covered up. Promise?"

Timmy adroitly changed the subject. He began to chant, quoting from the book his mother had been reading:

> *"Fuzzy Wuzzy was a bear.*
> *Fuzzy Wuzzy had no hair.*

*So Fuzzy Wuzzy wasn't fuzzy,
Was he?"*

Cherry tried to look stern. "Don't answer my question with another one. Are you going to obey orders while I'm gone?" She handed him the glass of pineapple juice.

"Straw," Timmy said tersely. "I *never* drink *any*thing without a straw."

For a moment Cherry almost lost her patience. It was getting on toward evening and she hadn't even unpacked. And where on this big, unfamiliar ship could she find a straw? Then she remembered the angled glass ones in the dispensary for patients who were not yet able to sit up. If she got one for Timmy it might keep him amused—it might even make it easier for his mother to force fluids. She darted away again to the dispensary.

And for the third time in the very same corridor on B deck she bumped into a passenger. This time it was not Jan Paulding. It was a tall, broad-shouldered man with a brown, weather-beaten face. But he, too, had been standing just outside of Stateroom 141; he hadn't known the door was going to be thrown open suddenly; like Jan he hadn't heard Cherry's rubber-soled shoes crossing the thick carpet.

But unlike Jan he was not surprised into near-panic when Cherry popped out into the corridor. Startled, yes, but he merely backed away with a suave apology:

"I beg your pardon, Nurse. I seem to have lost my way. This is where my cabin was when I last left it."

His sharp, bright-blue eyes twinkled merrily. "But *you* weren't in it when I went up to the club for tea."

His manner was pleasant enough, a trifle too molli-fying, Cherry thought, but there was something about his voice she didn't quite like. It was deep, almost harsh, as though he had overworked it, shouting com-mands, or uttering loud roars of uncontrollable rage.

He was wearing an immaculate tropical worsted suit of tiny brown and tan checks with an expensive-looking tie as bright as his twinkling eyes. But Cherry suspected he would feel more comfortable in something more rugged: a lumberjacket and dungarees, perhaps. He reminded her of a phrase the purser had used earlier that morn-ing describing the patient who had died in Curaçao: "A rough diamond, but a nice character."

Well, this man, Cherry felt sure, was another rough diamond. She didn't know whether he had a nice char-acter or not.

She smiled at him primly. "Perhaps you have the right room but the wrong deck. This is B deck."

"Oh, of course. How stupid of me." He shrugged his broad shoulders. "Do forgive me." He turned away toward the stairs. Cherry noted that his strides were long and that he moved with the muscular grace of an accomplished athlete.

"I don't believe for one minute he was lost," she told herself. "That man's too shrewd. He wouldn't lose his way in a labyrinth."

Later she glanced at the glass-framed deck plan on the wall in the dispensary. There were no cabins directly above the Cranes' and the doctor's suites. In that area on A deck were the gymnasium, the novelty shop, and the beauty salon.

There were no passenger staterooms except on A and B decks!

"The plot thickens," Cherry whispered to herself as she picked up a glass straw and locked herself out of the dispensary. "First the safe is broken into, hut nothing is taken. Next I catch Jan Paulding listening outside of Timmy's door. And now this extrapolite rough diamond, pretending he got his stateroom mixed up." And then she remembered something else.

They were heading into bad weather and the ship had rolled and pitched as the blue-eyed man strode down the corridor. Cherry had had a hard time keeping her balance just standing still, holding on to the dispensary door. But it hadn't fazed the mysterious passenger one bit. He had moved serenely along, as though enjoying the *Julita's* bucking motion. He had the most perfect pair of sea legs she had ever seen.

"My guess," she muttered, quoting Ziggy's description of the pulmonary thrombosis patient, "is that Mr. Rough Diamond has spent a lot of time at sea, during his youth and not too long ago either, because he couldn't be more than thirty-nine or forty now."

Soberly she let herself into Timmy's bedroom, wondering what could be the attraction No. 141 seemed to have for both Jan Paulding and Mr. Rough Diamond.

CHAPTER VI

~~~~~~

Scuttlebutt

TIMMY GREETED CHERRY WITH A GARBLED VERSION OF the ship's itinerary. Either his mother had foolishly misinformed him of the ports they would visit or he was deliberately making up a route of his own.

"We're going to Peru," he announced with an impish grin. "I know all about Peru." He began to chant:

> " *There was a young man from Peru,*
> *Who dreamed he was eating his shoe.*
> *He awoke in the night*
> *With a terrible fright*
> *To find it was perfectly true!'* "

Cherry laughed and went into the bathroom to wash the glass straw in hot, soapy water. Then she flushed it with alcohol and rinsed away the bitter taste. She taught Timmy how to drink his juice lying down. He thought it was great fun but preferred blowing bubbles.

At last Mrs. Crane took over. "I'll see that he drinks every drop of it," she promised Cherry. "We've taken up far too much of your time already."

"I've enjoyed it," Cherry said. "Just keep at the fluids, will you? He should have at least four ounces every half-hour, if possible." She sighed. She didn't envy helpless little Mrs. Crane the job of forcing fluids into mischievous young Timmy.

As she wearily left the room Timmy was pretending he was a whale and was spouting pineapple juice through the glass straw.

Back in her own little cabin she had hardly started to unpack when there was a tap at the door.

A young woman in a crisp, stewardess's uniform smiled at her in the dim light of the narrow passageway.

"I'm your neighbor in the next cabin," she told Cherry. "Helenita Browning is my name, but everybody calls me Brownie."

"I'm Cherry Ames, Brownie." They shook hands briefly. "Come in for a minute, won't you?" Cherry invited.

Brownie took one step across the threshold and then gave a gasp as she saw Cherry's Christmas presents spread out on the bed.

"Oh, how lovely," she cried, snatching up the red-rose taffeta bathing suit. "Yummy-yum, will you ever look lovely in this on the beach at Piscadera Bay."

"Piscadera Bay?"

Brownie nodded and draped the soft terry-cloth robe Cherry's mother had given her over her shoulders.

"That's at Curaçao. It's only a few minutes' bus drive from the port of Willemstad. If we can wangle shore leave at the same time, I'll show you the ropes."

As Cherry hung things in the closet, Brownie curled up on her bed, rambling on:

"Willemstad is a fascinating Dutch city; as picturesque as though a bit of Holland had been lifted out of Europe and set down smack in the Caribbean Sea. There's a fabulous pontoon bridge which swings back as ships come into the harbor. You'll get a big thrill when we sail right down the canal so close to the Hotel Americano you can almost touch the people sitting out on the veranda."

"Sounds like something out of a movie," Cherry said. "Tell me more, please."

"Well," Brownie went on willingly, "when people on the bridge see us coming they run like anything to get to shore because sometimes it stays open for more than half an hour. They can, of course, cross in *Verboot* which means ferryboat; it runs while the bridge is open. The buildings in Willemstad are fascinating; you'll love the eighteenth-century governor's palace and all the churches and the little bright-colored, gabled houses, pink and yellow stucco mostly. We'll visit the market where Venezuelan natives keep shop in boats along the shore."

Brownie scrambled to her feet. "We'd better get going. It must be time for dinner. You'll meet the other girls in this section then. They're all swell. We were wondering why you didn't show up for lunch."

As they left Cherry's stateroom, Brownie said in a carefully lowered voice, "Scuttlebutt says the purser's safe was broken into. Have you heard?"

"What do you mean, scuttlebutt?" Cherry asked.

"Oh, it's just a seagoing expression. Means the same as saying, 'Gossip hath.' The Old Man doesn't like gossip, so I'm not saying anything more. In fact," she admitted ruefully, "I don't *know* anything more. I'll bet it's just one of those yarns, anyway."

She tucked her arm through Cherry's as they strolled up to the promenade deck. Every now and then they lurched with the roll of the ship and almost tripped each other up.

"We're going to catch it tonight," Brownie said. "I pity you. Seasick passengers are a pain in the neck."

In the grill Cherry met three other stewardesses. They all sat at one big table and, ignoring the Captain's orders, gossiped throughout the meal. Cherry felt like a prig, but she could not violate her professional ethics and discuss Bill's accident. Nor did she divulge that she had been in the purser's office when Ziggy discovered the safe had been broken into.

"I wonder what was stolen," Miranda, a pretty young stewardess, kept asking. "That safe must be crammed full of jewelry. There are signs in every stateroom advising the passengers to check all valuables with the purser."

"If this little bit of scuttlebutt ever reaches the passengers' ears, the Old Man will have a fit," Brownie said. "Some of the women on this ship came aboard so laden down with platinum and diamonds under their mink coats I don't see how they managed to stagger up the gangplank."

Cherry saw Dr. Monroe dining at a near-by table with two ship's officers. He smiled at her swiftly with his eyes and then did not look in her direction again. Cherry knew that he must have heard the scuttlebutt by now and wondered if he suspected her of gossiping with the other girls.

Then she realized with relief that he couldn't do that, for she hadn't even mentioned it to him. And Ziggy must have told the ship's surgeon that Cherry was with him when he found the safe had been rifled.

"I was tempted to discuss the mystery with him," Cherry remembered. "But I'm glad I didn't."

Dinner over, the stewardesses hurried away to resume their duties. Cherry went down to the Crane suite, planning to stay with Timmy while his mother had her dinner in the big, *al fresco* dining room.

"It'll do you good to have a little change from these four walls," Cherry insisted when Mrs. Crane protested that she could eat on a tray with Timmy. "And don't hurry back. Timmy's due for another inhalation and more aspirin at eight anyway. I'll take his temperature then, too."

The word temperature decided Mrs. Crane. That was one thing she wasn't even going to attempt to cope with. She looked rather worn and harried after a long afternoon with a fretful little boy, and gratefully thanked Cherry for relieving her.

Cherry noticed with amusement that in spite of her exhaustion, pretty Mrs. Crane took the time to shower and change into a lovely, clinging evening gown of pale sea-green chiffon. When she was ready to go she leaned over the bed to kiss Timmy good-bye. But he pushed her away crossly:

"I don't like all that red stuff on your mouth. It gets all over me and my pajamas and the sheets. Then somebody might think I was a sissy."

Cherry quickly took in the fact that Timmy felt nowhere near as well as he had earlier. She laid her hand on his forehead and took his pulse. Yes, his temperature had undoubtedly gone up, but that was to be expected at this time of the evening. She called after Mrs. Crane:

"About what was his fluid intake? Did you manage to get a pint into him?"

"Oh, nothing like that," Mrs. Crane admitted. "He wouldn't take a thing after that one glass of pineapple juice. And he blew most of that all over the bed. I had to get a maid to change the sheets. They were soaked."

"Oh, dear," Cherry moaned inwardly. "Not enough fluid, and to make matters worse, Timmy probably was allowed out of bed while it was being changed."

Timmy, reading the despair on Cherry's face and correctly guessing the reason for it, began to sob. "Now, don't you scold me. I feel awful sick. I hurt all over."

He flipped around like a fish to bury his face in the pillows. "I want my Nanny," he kept wailing. "She *never* scolds me. Don't you try to make me drink water. I *hate* water. When I *have* to have it, Nanny feeds it to me with a spoon and tells me stories all the time."

Cherry tried to comfort him, deciding that she would not wait until eight to take his temperature. She would take it just as soon as he quieted down.

"Don't cry, Timmy," she said soothingly. "I'll feed you water with a spoon and tell you stories too."

Immediately, he flipped back to grin up at her. "Okey-dokey. Go get the nasty old water and a spoon. But your stories better be good or I won't swallow a drop."

Rain was splattering against the windows that opened out on the deck. Cherry hoped that Timmy wasn't going to be seasick along with his cold. The deck heaved beneath her feet and she almost spilled the water she brought from the bathroom. But Timmy didn't seem to mind the *Julita's* jerky progress at all.

Cherry told him stories until she was almost as hoarse as he was, but in the end she managed to spoon four ounces of water into him and six ounces of prune juice.

When she finally took his temperature she found it had risen to 103°. She must consult Dr. Monroe at once. He would probably want to start Timmy on sulfa at eight instead of the aspirin. It was almost eight now, and she was due in sick bay for Bill's regular check. When would Mrs. Crane come back?

In desperation she rang the steward's bell. "I hope it doesn't bring Waidler," she mumbled. But it did.

"Well?" he scowled from the doorway. "What does your highness want now?"

Cherry blinked back tears of exhaustion and anxiety. "Please, Waidler," she begged, "will you go and get Mrs. Crane? I imagine she's still at dinner. I have to go down to sick bay for a few minutes."

"What's stopping you?" he demanded sourly. "Don't tell me this little bit of motion has thrown you off your feet. Wait until tonight. If you can't walk now you'll be a big help when the passengers start sending for you."

Cherry sucked in a deep breath. "It's not the rough seas," she said quietly. "I can't leave this little boy alone. He's running quite a bit of temperature. Please, get his mother."

Waidler merely glared at her. And then, miraculously, Timmy came to the rescue. "Tell me a story, please, Mr. Waidler," he said. "Tell me a story about pirates."

Cherry felt sorry for innocent little Timmy who took it for granted that everyone was his friend. "That old sea dog, Waidler, probably *does* know some swell yarns," she thought. "But he wouldn't waste a minute of his precious time amusing a sick little boy."

"Oh, all right, all *right,*" Waidler was mumbling gruffly. "Go long, Nurse. But don't get it into your head that sitting with your patients is one of my duties. If the Captain ever heard about this—" He shook his head darkly. "No good will come of it. Mark my words!"

But Timmy merely wriggled ecstatically, and patted a spot beside him on the bed. "Sit down here, Mr. Waidler. I *have* to know all about pirates."

Cherry fled, thinking, "If anyone can get under Waidler's barnacled shell it will be Timmy. No one could resist that lovable little imp!"

CHAPTER VII

A Stormy Night

WHEN CHERRY BREATHLESSLY ARRIVED IN SICK BAY, Dr. Monroe was ahead of her, taking Bill's T.P.R.

"Oh, dear," she sighed inwardly. "Now I'm in for it. And the very first night at sea!"

But Dr. Kirk Monroe only looked up and smiled. "You needn't have come down, Miss Ames. I saw Mrs. Crane dancing in the club and guessed you were tied up with Timmy." His stethoscope was dangling from his neck, and his fingers, which had been on Bill's pulse, looked cool and capable. He said reassuringly, "This patient is doing fine. But I'm going to have Rick sleep in the upper bunk tonight. How's our other patient?"

Cherry, still a little flustered from hurrying, said, "His temperature is up two degrees, Doctor. And Tim aches all over. Looks like incipient influenza to me."

Rick came into sick bay then, and Dr. Monroe left with Cherry shortly afterward. On the way up to

B deck Cherry thought he might mention the mystery of the purser's safe, but he didn't.

As they entered the Crane suite Waidler was obviously in the middle of an exciting tale of adventure on the high seas.

"Go 'way, you two," Timmy yelled petulantly. "Waidy's telling me about Henry Morgan who was the most froshus pirate of 'em all."

So it was "Waidy" now! Cherry could hardly suppress a chuckle. The steward's face turned crimson as he stumbled to his feet.

Dr. Monroe said easily, "Thank you, Waidler. It was very co-operative of you to help us out." To Timmy, he said: "I have a book in my cabin. It's full of pirate stories and I think you'll like the pictures. Perhaps Miss Ames will read to you while you're being steamed."

"Who's Miss *Sames?*" Timmy demanded.

The young ship's doctor looked puzzled. Then he laughed. "Oh, I meant to say *Cherry* would read it."

Timmy sank back against the pillows in relief. "That's dif-frunt. She's okay, but her stories aren't very 'citing. Not like *his.*" He pointed a fat finger at Waidler who was trying to creep unobtrusively away. "When *he* was a little boy he was captured by pirates. But he got away 'cause he chopped off their heads one by one with a great big 'normous knife."

The steward disappeared so quickly it seemed as though he must have melted through the door. Cherry let the laughter bubble up to her lips.

Dr. Kirk Monroe laughed too. "That Waidler!" he said in an aside to Cherry. "He's a character. He's got a terrific bark but no bite at all. At the beginning of every cruise we're swamped with complaints from the passengers about his attitude. And in the end they all fraternize with him outrageously."

"Why does he pose as such a disagreeable person?" Cherry asked curiously.

"I couldn't tell you. That's a problem for psychiatry." Dr. Monroe smiled. He listened to Timmy's chest, thumped his back, and then sat back and stared at him for a long minute. More to himself than to Cherry he said: "For the present, we'll keep him on the same routine. After his inhalation we'll give him five grains of aspirin and a teaspoon of elixir of Luminal. That should keep him quiet throughout the night."

"Yes, Doctor," Cherry said. "About his diet. Apparently he's had nothing since breakfast."

"I'm not hungry," Timmy howled. "I *won't* eat!"

Dr. Monroe said gently, "And you don't have to, Tim. Not if you drink a big chocolate milk shake." To Cherry, he added quietly: "Put a raw egg in it."

And then he was gone. Everything went smoothly, and Timmy was tucked in bed, drowsy-eyed, when his mother came back. Mrs. Crane's eyes were sparkling. She had, obviously, had a good time.

Cherry said that Tim very probably would sleep until morning, but that Mrs. Crane should not hesitate to call the doctor if he seemed worse.

"I do hope I won't get seasick," Mrs. Crane said worriedly. "One of the women at our table in the club left rather hurriedly a few minutes ago. I imagine you've got another patient."

Mrs. Crane was right. Out in the corridor the loudspeaker was calling:

"Nurse Ames. Nurse Ames. Report to Dr. Monroe in Stateroom 17. Stateroom 17. Nurse Ames."

Stateroom 17. That must be on A deck. Cherry hurried up the stairs.

From then on it was a nightmare. Cherry was called to one suite after another all night long. Fretful, frightened people. Pampered women who refused to listen to reason. Some of them, convinced that the ship was going to roll and pitch for the entire twelve days, insisted upon being taken off at once. Others, giving way to the nausea, had to be coaxed for long minutes into chewing the little candy-coated pieces of gum.

Cherry was so busy she hardly noticed the heaving decks and the thudding splash of rain against the windowpanes. But at last it was morning, a heaven-sent, sunny dawn. Cherry thought she had never appreciated balmy weather so much before in all her life.

Then the "convalescents" had to be wheedled into sipping hot tea and munching thin pieces of hard toast or crackers. Cherry explained over and over again: "You're very dehydrated. You must take a little fluid every fifteen or twenty minutes. This nice dry toast will help settle your stomach. Really, it will. Please try."

At seven, Dr. Monroe ordered her to breakfast. "It's all over now," he said. Cherry noticed the deep circles under his eyes and wondered if she looked as drawn and tired. Apparently she did, for he said sternly:

"Have a big, hot, leisurely breakfast. The stewards and stewardesses will take over from here on in. After you have charted our two real patients' T.P.R., you are to take a nap. Doctor's orders."

"Yes, Doctor." Cherry smiled wanly. Dazed with exhaustion and lack of sleep, she somehow managed to get down creamy oatmeal, drenched in brown sugar and thick cream. Then the waitress brought fluffy scrambled eggs and a cup of cocoa. Cherry propped her eyes open and finished everything. She knew nourishment meant renewed strength. You could never tell what the day might bring forth.

Bill, fortunately, as he said himself, was as good as new except for the use of his right arm. But Timmy's condition was unchanged. Cherry had expected—hoped that his early morning temperature would be near normal. She was sleepily scribbling notes which she would later enter in the sick bay log, when Dr. Monroe came in.

"That settles it," he said, when Cherry handed him her pad. "We have a new sulfa compound which I'll have sent in to you at once. First dose, four tablets; subsequent doses, two every four hours. Day and night."

Mrs. Crane, still surprised that she had managed to sleep through the stormy night, hovered closer. "Oh, doctor, what is it? Not pneu-pneumonia?"

Dr. Monroe immediately assured her, "Nothing of the kind. It's a simple case of laryngitis with some inflammation of the trachea." He hurried away.

Tim's mother looked more horrified than ever. Cherry explained quietly, "In other words, Mrs. Crane, just plain croup. Doctor is putting Timmy on sulfa merely as a precaution against a further rise in temperature. He may respond to the first dose and run no more fever."

Mrs. Crane said, relieved, "Oh, croup. Timmy has had croup on and off since he was born. Nanny says the pediatrician told her he was just one of those children who are extremely susceptible to croup." She blew an airy little kiss to Timmy and went off to breakfast.

Cherry couldn't help thinking: "So the pediatrician told *Nanny* that! Where was Timmy's mother at the time?" She shook her head. "Probably out dancing somewhere. Poor little Tim! If ever a boy needed a real mother, this one does. Lots of his crankiness is due to the fact that he feels insecure. He demands attention as a compensation. He's not really spoiled—he's just starving for mother love."

And yet, Mrs. Crane was a nice woman. And she *was* fond of Timmy. Why couldn't she see that he had outgrown a nanny and needed *her?*

Ziggy himself brought the sulfa tablets from the dispensary. He said with a grin, "Waidler has got the refrigerator in my office bulging with provisions. I signed a requisition a mile long. You should see your own desk. There are neat little stacks of bouillon cubes, tea bags, and heaven knows what all, reaching right up to the overhead."

So Waidler was over his grouch. Maybe he was like those people who were always grouchy in the morning. Maybe Waidler felt about the first day at sea as they did about the first few minutes before breakfast.

Ziggy pointed to Cherry's rumpled uniform. "I'd say you'd slept in your clothes except that I know better. You look as though you were going to fall asleep on your feet any minute. Want me to send a stewardess in here to relieve you while you catch a little shut-eye?"

Timmy arched his back in rage. "Don't want anybody 'cept Cherry."

Cherry smiled her thanks at the purser. "I won't be through with this little patient for another half hour anyway. By that time his mother should be back from breakfast. But thanks for thinking about me."

Ziggy produced a toothpick and chewed on it while Cherry, using the dispensary mortar and pestle he had thoughtfully brought in, pounded four of the sulfa tablets into a powder. She mixed this powder with the strained prunes on Timmy's ignored breakfast tray.

"Have a compliment for you, Miss Cherry," Ziggy said gruffly. "When I was telling Doc that you were among those present when I discovered the, er—shall we say accident, in my office yesterday, he seemed right pleased that you had neglected to report same to him. Says he to me, 'Miss Cherry is one of those rare combinations of beauty and the beast.' Or was it beauty and brains?" Ziggy fled, embarrassed at the slip of his tongue.

Cherry laughed, thankful that she had resisted the temptation to gossip. Timmy promptly sat up. "Tell me the story of 'Beauty and the Beast,' Cherry. I have a bear, too. Only he's not a 'chanted prince. He's a fuzzy-wuzzy bear. But I losted him, so p'raps he's not fuzzy-wuzzy any more."

Cherry could not suppress a weary yawn. "That's too bad, Timmy," she got out in the middle of the yawn. "Now if you eat up every speck of your prunes I'll tell you the story of 'Beauty and the Beast.' "

Patiently she spooned the fruit and sulfa mixture into him and started the vaporizer going. From inside his tent, Timmy said excitedly:

"Tomorrow's Christmas Eve. Waidy says we're going to have a big tree in the *liberry*. I'm going to get all well quick so I can see it. 'N' I'm going to hang up my stocking by the fireplace in the great big living room. It's a fake fireplace," he confided with ill-disguised disgust, "but Waidy says Santa Claus knows about ships so he's going to come down the smokestack."

Cherry jerked herself out of a half doze. Tomorrow was not only Christmas Eve. It was her birthday, and Charlie's too! A lump swelled in her throat as she thought of her family. Thank goodness they couldn't know what a hectic day and night she had just lived through! How Dr. Joe would scold if he knew she had been on duty almost constantly for the past twenty hours!

Cherry unplugged the vaporizer and removed the tent. Now that Timmy was on sulfa his fluid intake per hour must not be less than eight ounces. They must not risk the effect of the powerful drug on the little boy's system if he refused to absorb a sufficient amount of liquid. How could she depend upon his mother to force even four ounces of fluid while Cherry had her long-anticipated nap?

She couldn't. She herself must somehow spoon a full eight ounces into him before she went off duty. By now Cherry was indeed almost "asleep on her feet." She hated to leave the little boy alone while she raced up to the purser's office on A deck for a can of ice-cold juice. But neither did she feel right about again calling on Waidler for help. She wasn't quite sure how Dr. Monroe felt about that. He hadn't seemed annoyed, but he had dismissed the steward rather quickly. Perhaps she had unknowingly violated some shipboard regulation.

And there was no telling when Mrs. Crane would come back. The sunbathed decks, swept by warm, salty breezes, would be a great temptation. So would the happy crowd that must have gathered by now around the green tiled pool.

Cherry made up her mind; she would have to risk it. To Timmy she said, coaxingly, "You're a big boy, going on seven. So I'm sure I can leave you alone for a few minutes, can't I?"

Timmy nodded soberly.

"You won't get out of bed, no matter what happens? Promise?"

Timmy hesitated. "No. Won't promise. Not 'less you leave the door open. 'Pose my mummy comes back and can't get in? She *never* 'members to bring her key."

Leaving the door to the corridor open, Cherry decided quickly, might be the wisest thing to do. If she were delayed for some reason and Timmy wanted something, he could call out to a passing steward.

She propped the door open and then remembered what had happened to the purser's safe yesterday. Mrs. Crane was just the type to leave money and jewelry carelessly lying around. Cherry's dark eyes swiftly swept the bedroom and the adjoining living room. Nothing of value was in sight.

With a parting admonition to Timmy that he must not get out of bed, she sped down the corridor. Halfway to the staircase she passed the same spot where she had first bumped into slim, blonde Jan. The door she had popped out of yesterday was slightly ajar, Cherry noticed incuriously. The number on the door was 125, the bedroom of Suite 125-127.

Then she suddenly became curious. As she hurried by, someone standing just inside the bedroom swiftly closed the door. Someone in a colorful dirndl skirt.

A dirndl skirt, Cherry felt sure, was exactly what tiny waisted young Jan Paulding would be wearing on this bright, almost tropical day!

But Cherry was too tired to wonder much about that then. Up on A deck she saw some of her patients of the night before. Only a few of them smiled in recognition, and none of them looked really robust. One passenger, however, in the crowd that was milling toward the swimming pool, looked extremely healthy. She could only see his broad back in a tannish gabardine suit, but she would have known that almost swaggering gait anywhere.

He turned as though feeling her eyes upon him, and she caught a glimpse of his tanned face as she whisked into the purser's office. Mr. Rough Diamond was not feeling any ill effects of the stormy night; Mr. Rough Diamond felt fine and very sure of himself.

CHAPTER VIII

Timmy's Mysterious Visitor

FATE, IT SEEMED, ALWAYS CONSPIRED TO DELAY CHERRY whenever she was in a hurry. This time, Fate took the simple form of a common garden-variety can opener. The refrigerator was, as Ziggy had reported, crammed with all kinds of canned juices. But there was nothing, absolutely nothing, to open them with.

"If this were only an old-fashioned icebox," Cherry wailed. "An old-fashioned ice pick is all I ask for at this moment."

At last she discovered, far back in the refrigerator, a small bottle of apple juice. She had seen a wall attachment for opening bottles in Timmy's bathroom. Prayerfully she hoped that he liked apple juice. One consolation was that, while poking around on the shelves, she had discovered a box of bright colored straws. Perhaps Timmy would enjoy sucking the juice straight from the bottle. Cherry remembered that she had spurned glasses when she was his age. Midge still did.

Cherry carefully locked the door to the purser's office behind her and raced back to her patient. She skidded to a stop as she crossed the threshold to Timmy's room. She gasped in chagrin. Toys of all sizes and descriptions were heaped helter-skelter on his bed. The closet door stood open and the bottom drawers had been yanked out. Toys and shoes spilled out of them: stuffed animals, rubber animals, plastic animals, books, trains, boats—Nanny or somebody must have packed a trunkful of everything in Timmy's nursery at home.

And there could be only one answer to the topsy-turvy room. Timmy had disobeyed orders. Cherry should never have left him alone. She should have known that she couldn't rely on a six-year-old's promise.

She blinked back tears and, shutting the door, marched to his bedside. "Timmy Crane," she began sternly. "You got out of bed. You broke your promise."

Timmy, brown eyes wide with innocence, stared at her. "I *never* break my promise," he said with convincing dignity.

Cherry confronted him with a grinning stuffed elephant. "Then how did Mr. Elephant get from your toy box to your bed. And don't you dare tell me he walked!"

Timmy laughed as only a mischievous small boy can laugh. " 'Course, Elly didn't walk," he finally got out. "Elly can't walk, silly. He's too fat to walk. You're just as silly as that girl who threw him to me when I asked her for my duck."

Cherry sat down hard on the foot of his bed. "What girl?" she asked weakly.

Timmy squirmed with delight. He knew something Cherry didn't know. "*That* girl," he shouted. "The one with long yellow pigtails on top of her head." He grinned impishly. " 'Cept they didn't *stay* on top of her head when she was trying to find my duck. They came tumbling down and she looked just like the girl in the storybook. The one who hung her pigtails out of the window so somebody could climb up."

Jan Paulding! Cherry's numb mind couldn't take in anything more.

"She's kind of nice, Cherry," Timmy went on gleefully, "but awful silly. She threw me 'most everything in those drawers 'cept my duck. And there it was, plain as could be." He pointed to the strewn floor around the closet. Sure enough, the fluffy little yellow duck *was* in plain view.

"And she's an awful fraidy-cat too," Timmy told Cherry. "When she looked up and saw that man watching her, she sat right down on top of my 'lectric train and sort of breathed funny like Mummy does when she's going to cry."

"A man, Timmy? What man?" Cherry asked Timmy in a faint voice.

"The *nice* man, Cherry," Timmy shouted hoarsely.

Cherry realized then that she should not let him talk so much. His face was flushed and he punctuated his story with sharp little coughs.

"Never mind, Timmy," she said soothingly. "You can tell me all about it later. I've got some juice for you. You can drink it right out of the bottle with this long, red straw."

Whatever had happened in Room 141 during her absence, it had at least made Timmy thirsty. He sucked up the last drops of apple juice with loud "glurping" noises of satisfaction. Then he insisted upon continuing the conversation. Cherry offered to read instead, but he stuck his fingers in his ears. She tried to tell him what she knew about Morgan, the bloodthirsty pirate. Instead of listening he thrashed around in bed and pulled the pillow down over his face.

Unfortunately, the ship's surgeon, refreshed from a short nap, chose that moment to tap on the door. Dr. Monroe was in whites now and he looked very handsome, but Cherry wished with all her heart that he had slept a little longer.

His gray eyes swept the topsy-turvy room. They took in Cherry's rumpled, prune-stained uniform and came to rest on the red-faced boy in the topsy-turvy, toy-heaped bed.

"What *is* going on here?" His voice was husky with annoyance and surprise.

Timmy wailed at the top of his lungs: "She won't listen to me. She wants to do all the talking. She talks and talks and *talks!* Make her listen to *me!*"

Dr. Monroe frowned. "It seems to me, Miss Ames," he said, "that you mentioned once you were pretty good with sick little boys. If this is an example—" He spread his hands expressively.

Cherry's taut nerves snapped under the sting of sarcasm in his voice. She stood in front of him, hands clinched tightly at her sides. "Your criticism, Dr. Monroe, is entirely unfair. I apologize for my impertinence; you force me to defend myself, and I shall. The patient has done far too much talking already. He has been coughing almost incessantly, is very hoarse, and extremely overstimulated. If you ask my opinion, and I know you won't, I would tell you—"

Afterward, Cherry realized that nervous exhaustion had goaded her into making such an unprofessional scene. But she did not regret a word she said. And surprisingly, instead of resenting her insubordination, Dr. Monroe threw back his head and roared with laughter.

"Cherry Ames!" he exploded. "I admire your spunk. And," he added more soberly, "I shouldn't have listened to the patient's complaint. You *don't* talk too much. I found that out yesterday."

Cherry bit her lip to keep from bursting into tears. First a scolding and now a compliment! It was too much of a rightabout-face for her!

"You run along to bed, Nur—Cherry," he said kindly. "I'll give the boy some Cheracol myself and get a maid to clean up this mess."

Cherry fled. He had called her by her first name! Had he done it simply because he felt sorry for her? Or had he called her Cherry because he thought of her as a human being, not just his nurse? It was nice to think that the latter premise was true. And thinking about it, she fell into an exhausted sleep.

When her alarm clock jangled an hour later she sat up dazedly. At first she didn't know where she was, had forgotten she was aboard an ocean liner. The tiny cabin, which she had hardly glimpsed since coming aboard, was coldly impersonal. The throbbing of the engines blended with the dull ache in her head.

Then it all came flooding back—Timmy's wild tale that she had deliberately interrupted. How much of it was fact; how much fantasy? His description of the girl with the long blond braids fitted Jan Paulding exactly. Had she been watching from her stateroom door, waiting for a moment when Timmy would be alone in his suite?

And who was the man—the *nice* man?

Someone tapped on her door. It was Brownie, the plump young stewardess. "Lunch in ten minutes," she said. Taking in Cherry's disheveled appearance, she added, "Oh, 'scuse it, please. I didn't know you were sleeping."

Cherry scrambled to her feet. "You didn't wake me up. I had to get up, anyway. I've got to check on two patients at noon." Hurriedly she whitened her shoes, showered and changed into a fresh uniform and cap. Brownie, idly examining the snapshots Cherry had tucked around her mirror, asked:

"Who's the handsome lad in the pilot's uniform? I could go for him."

"That's my twin brother," Cherry told her. "Charlie."

"Oh, boy," Brownie said enthusiastically. "I hope he comes aboard sometime when I'm around. Will he meet you when we dock after the cruise?"

"I'm afraid not." Cherry smiled. "We live in Illinois, you see."

Brownie cheerfully shrugged away her disappointed hopes. "Speaking of handsome lads," she said, as they hurried to lunch, "that boss of yours makes my heart go pitapat every time I pass him in the corridor. Of course, he doesn't even know I exist. Awfully dignified, isn't he?"

Cherry didn't know what to reply. Anything she said would come under the head of gossiping. At last she compromised with "He's a fine surgeon."

"Oh, *you!*" Brownie squeezed Cherry's arm impatiently. "Don't you ever break down and stop being a stiffly starched, registered nurse?"

Cherry, remembering all of the scrapes she had been involved in since her student days, couldn't help laughing.

"You don't *look* stiffly starched," Brownie went on in her friendly way. "Everybody keeps saying how pretty you are, and the girls are all jealous of your red cheeks and that naturally curly hair."

"Those same red cheeks," Cherry laughed, "almost got me expelled from Nurses' Training School. The chief surgeon kept ordering me to wipe off the rouge. And I couldn't."

Brownie giggled. "I guess you're human after all."

Lunch was creamed mushrooms on toast with *pu-réed* spinach and a crisp salad. "One thing I'll say about this line," Brownie whispered. "They feed us the same things they give the passengers." She helped herself to two large pieces of French pastry. "I always gain about five pounds every cruise."

After lunch, Cherry did her routine check on Bill, interrupting the game of checkers he was playing with one of his buddies who was off duty until four o'clock. He made faces at her all the time the thermometer was in his mouth, twitching his nose and wriggling his eyebrows.

Cherry, her fingers on his pulse, pursed her lips with mock severity. She felt rested and strong again, and wondered how she could have delivered such a tirade of impertinence to the ship's surgeon only two hours ago.

After charting her bedside notes she hurried up to Timmy. Proudly he waved to an array of bottles on a table within easy reach.

"Mine," he announced loftily. "Every one of 'em. Kirk gave 'em to me and this shiny new opener so I can pry off the tops myself. Soon as I have 'nuff bottle tops he's going to teach me how to play checkers with 'em."

Kirk! Timmy certainly believed in the use of first names. Kirk—what a nice name! And how it fitted this serious-minded, soft-spoken man.

"Also," Timmy went on while she took his temperature, "there's something dif-frunt in every one of those bottles. Orange, lemon, lime, apple, pineapple, prune, apricot, even one named after you, Cherry."

Dr. Monroe, Cherry decided, had a way with little boys. He understood their desire to "do" for themselves. She took the thermometer to the French doors leading out on deck and read the verdict. Temperature unchanged. Well, you couldn't expect a miracle right away.

"Also," Timmy said again, trying to regain her attention. "Also" was a new word Timmy had picked up somewhere and he intended to work it to death. "Also, Kirk said I was to tell you the story of the man and the duck. Kirk thought it was a very funny story. You'll laugh like anything, Cherry."

Cherry, busy with mortar and pestle, said vaguely, "All right, tell me the story."

"Well," Timmy began, enjoying the reversed role of teller of tales instead of listener, "first that girl couldn't find my duck. Then she sat down on my train and 'most cried when she saw that man staring at her." Cherry pricked up her ears. "*And* the man was 'most as silly as the girl, Cherry. Do you know what he asked the girl? He said, sort of smiling, 'Looking for something?' Wasn't that silly? 'Course she was looking for something. She was looking for my duck! *And* 'stead of telling him that, she just jumped up and ran away. So then I told the man to please give me my duck. I said *please* 'cause he's so big and strong looking. He 'minded me of the pirates in Dr. Kirk's book. Not the bad ones. The nice ones, Cherry."

He rambled on between spoonfuls of the strained fruit and sulfa mixture, hardly knowing that Cherry was feeding him. Cherry listened attentively. The man with the nice pirate face, she began to suspect, was Mr. Rough Diamond. Perhaps she was on the verge of discovering why he and Jan were so interested in Stateroom 141.

Mrs. Crane, who had been resting in the adjoining living room, called out:

"Don't let the child bore you to death, Miss Ames. He's apt to let his imagination run away with him."

Bored! Cherry couldn't have been more interested. She was delighted that her boss had "ordered" her to listen to Timmy's tale.

"*So,* after I said *please* two more times, he laughed and came inside the room, and then *he* began to look. But he couldn't find the duck either. Course he looked in all the wrong places. Like where Waidy put our empty suitcases, 'way back on top of the closet. *And* just everywhere 'cept the right place. While he was looking, Cherry, he told me all about the place where we're going to stop first. So I didn't mind so much not having my duck."

Timmy sat up in bed wide-eyed. "Do you know what, Cherry? We're going to sail right down the middle of a city. Right down a canal—that's a water street," he explained painstakingly. "The man said we'd pass so close to people on shore I can spit on 'em. Won't that be fun?"

"That will be fun," Cherry agreed. She added shrewdly: "So he left without *finding* anything?"

Timmy shook his head vigorously up and down. "But he promised to come back and tell me about the man with the wooden leg."

"Another pirate?" Cherry asked.

"No, he was a Dutchman. Peter Stuy-Stuy—anyway, his *first* name was Peter. He got hurt fighting the Indians. So they had to chop off his leg. *And* it's buried right there where we're going to stop first. Cura-something or other."

"Curaçao," Cherry finished. "And I imagine the man with the wooden leg was Peter Stuyvesant, wasn't he?"

Timmy stared at her incredulously. "Do *you* know about him, too?"

"Not very much," Cherry admitted with a laugh. It was obvious that Timmy preferred people who related the bloodthirsty events of history. "Do you want me to read you some of the pirate stories in the book Dr. Monroe loaned you?"

Timmy whooped with joy. Mrs. Crane came into the bedroom. "If you're going to read for a while, I think I'll take a swim. Mind?"

"No, indeed." Cherry smiled. "I'm as interested in hearing about the pirates who roamed the Caribbean as Timmy is."

Timmy would listen to nothing but tales of the wicked Henry Morgan. Cherry found out that this wily pirate had succeeded in getting himself knighted and at one time was deputy governor of Jamaica.

They were in the midst of an exciting description of Morgan's brilliant and daring capture of Maracaibo from the Spaniards, when someone tapped on the door.

Cherry was surprised to see that it was Jan Paulding. Cherry frowned. Had the young girl been listening outside the door again? If so, such snooping certainly deserved a scolding. Cherry made up her mind to have a talk with Jan Paulding before the day was over.

CHAPTER IX

Uncle Ben

JAN PAULDING, IN TAILORED SHARKSKIN SLACKS AND a fuchsia sweater, was tautly poised. To Cherry she looked as nervous as a little girl about to give her first public recital.

"Oh, Miss Ames," she said, in a clear, cool voice. "I thought I would find you here. Would you mind stepping down the hall a minute to our suite? Mother has a ghastly headache." She waved with forced airiness to Timmy. "I'll be glad to stay with your little patient."

Cherry shook her head, smiling. "I'm sorry, but I can't. It's against the rules. I'm not allowed to give nursing care except by order of the ship's surgeon."

A flash of something akin to anger flickered in Jan's huge hazel eyes. She said coldly, "But that's perfectly ridiculous. Dr. Monroe stopped in shortly after lunch and said he would send you immediately with aspirin and an ice bag. When you didn't show up, I decided to come after you." She frowned. "Mother is really ill."

"I'm sorry, but I can't leave my patient," Cherry repeated. "Why don't you send for a steward and have the doctor paged on the loud-speaker? He'll go to your suite at once, unless he's tied up with a more serious case."

Jan clenched her slim fingers into tight fists. "I tell you it *is* serious. When Mother gets those blinding headaches she almost goes crazy. She threatens to—to—well, hurt herself if she doesn't get prompt relief. And I did tell that crosspatch steward to get Dr. Monroe. Half an hour ago."

Cherry was torn now between duty to a patient and the rules and regulations. Dr. Monroe might well be tied up with a really serious case. If so, he would certainly expect her to take over the minor cases until he was free. What harm could there be in leaving Timmy with this lovely young girl while she slipped down the corridor for a minute or two?

No harm at all, Cherry decided. She turned to the little boy. "Timmy, this is Miss Jan Paulding. She's got a sick mother who needs me. Is it all right if I leave you with Jan for a few minutes?"

"Hello, silly," Timmy greeted Jan impolitely. "Catch!" With a friendly grin he tossed the soft yellow duck to Jan's outstretched hands. *"That's* what I wanted you to find this morning."

Cherry left them laughing together and sped down to the Paulding suite. Jan had left the bedroom door ajar. Her mother, a fat, pasty-faced woman, was clasping a wet towel to her forehead.

"Nurse, Nurse," she moaned. "Do something."

Cherry said quietly, "Haven't you a prescription from your own physician that relieves these headaches?"

"Of course," Mrs. Paulding groaned. "A sedative and painkiller in a liquid form. But I dropped the bottle on the bathroom floor last night during the storm." She writhed under the sheet. "Codein and aspirin, please. I can't stand the pain another minute."

"I'm sorry," Cherry said, with genuine sympathy. "I'm not allowed to give any medication without an order from Dr. Monroe. He'll be along any minute, I'm sure. Let me fix you an ice bag in the meantime."

Without waiting for a reply she raced up to the purser's office for ice cubes, then back down to the dispensary for an ice bag. Then down the corridor to Suite 125-127. Both times, as she passed Timmy's door, she noticed that it was closed, although she had left it open.

Dr. Monroe was sitting beside Mrs. Paulding's bed when Cherry hurried into the room. He glanced briefly at Cherry and took the ice bag from her. "That will be all, Nurse. I'm going to give Mrs. Paulding a sixth of morphine."

She was glad to leave it at that. Mrs. Paulding would soon be free from pain and certainly Cherry had done nothing wrong.

She had to knock twice on Timmy's door before Jan opened it. Cherry took one look and froze in her tracks. Everywhere were signs that the room had been searched again. The furniture had been moved slightly from against the walls. A chair stood beside the open closet. The rug had been rolled away and hastily but not smoothly rolled back.

Timmy said happily, "She's looking for Fuzzy-Wuzzy now. But she'll never find him. Not in *here!*"

Cherry took two swift strides across the room and grabbed Jan's wrist. "Jan Paulding," she said sternly, "I'm ashamed of you. Using your mother's illness as an excuse to illegally search another passenger's room."

Jan burst into tears and crumpled down on the empty twin bed. "I wouldn't take anything that didn't belong to me," she wailed. "I only want what's mine. My very own."

Cherry refused to weaken. "Talk sense," she said crisply. "Why should anything that belonged to you be in Timmy's bedroom?"

Jan raised her tearstained face. "Plenty, that's what," she cried. "And it's none of your business, Miss Ames."

Cherry felt like spanking the girl—hard. "Now, you listen to me, Jan Paulding," she said firmly. "It is so much my business that unless you explain yourself I shall report you to the ship's surgeon. He, in turn, will report you to the captain. And then you will be in trouble."

Jan sat up abruptly and crossed her long, slender legs. "All right, I'll explain. But you've got to promise not to tell anybody else."

Cherry shook her head. "I won't promise anything of the kind. I shall certainly report you at once unless you give me good and sufficient reason for what amounts to your breaking and entering."

At that moment Mrs. Crane came back from her swim. She nodded vaguely to Jan. It turned out that Mrs. Crane and the Pauldings were seated at the same table in the dining room.

Jan stood up and said quickly, "Oh, Mrs. Crane. I stopped by to get the nurse for Mother. She's quite ill. Is it all right if Miss Ames leaves Timmy with you now?"

"Why, of course," Timmy's mother said. "We don't own Miss Ames. I'm sorry about your mother. Let me know if I can do anything."

"The Cranes may not own me," Cherry thought amusedly, "but Jan Paulding acts as though she did." Out in the corridor she said: "If your mother is sleeping, perhaps we can have a little talk in the other room."

"That's right," Jan said. "She will be asleep. She always goes to sleep the minute the pain is relieved."

"Why are you so sure the pain has been relieved?" Cherry demanded suspiciously.

Jan shrugged. "The doctor arrived soon after you, didn't he?"

Cherry nodded. "So, to add to your other crimes, you lied to me?"

"I did not," Jan insisted. "Dr. Monroe did stop by right after lunch. Mother sent for him because she broke her bottle of medicine. She was afraid she might get one of those headaches. He told her that if she did he would send you to her at once with aspirin and an ice bag if he himself couldn't come right away."

"I see." Cherry thought for a minute. "What about Waidler, the steward? You told me you sent him for the doctor half an hour ago."

"That was perfectly true too," Jan said defiantly. "That was at two o'clock. I told him to ask Dr. Monroe to stop in at two-thirty. It takes Mother that long to work herself up into a real state of excitement."

Jan led Cherry into Room 127, the living room of the suite. "You sound like an awfully hardhearted daughter to me," Cherry said. She peeked through the door between the two rooms and saw that Mrs. Crane was sleeping peacefully.

Jan began to cry again. "You don't know my mother or you wouldn't say that. She—she *likes* being sick. You'll find that out before the cruise is over. Wait and see."

Cherry began to weaken. Either Jan Paulding was an accomplished actress or she was a thoroughly unhappy young girl. And the glimpse Cherry had had of Mrs. Paulding had not made her feel that she was an admirable or sympathetic mother. Mrs. Paulding had been in pain, of course. But Cherry had nursed lots of other people in pain too. Very few of them had whined and moaned and groaned.

She drew a chair up to the sofa and patted Jan's shaking shoulders. "Come on, honey," she said gently. "Crying isn't going to do any good. Sit up and tell me all about it."

Jan sat up and wiped her streaming eyes with a brightly checkered handkerchief. "It's the ambergris," she blurted. "I *have* to find it. Don't you see? It's the only way I can go to art school."

Cherry didn't see and said so. "You'd better begin at the beginning. You might start alphabetically with the letter A, for ambergris. All I know about it is that it's used in the manufacture of perfume even though it's supposed to smell horrible. It's formed in the intestines of whales, isn't it?"

A smile lighted up Jan's teary face. "That's all I knew about it, too." She giggled. "Until Uncle Ben arrived. Oh, Cherry, let me tell you about ambergris. Sailors call it 'Fool's Gold of the Sea,' because they're always finding something that *isn't* ambergris. Real ambergris is absolutely priceless!"

Cherry glanced at her wrist watch. "It sounds fascinating, but I haven't too much time. Maybe you had better give me the story of ambergris some other time. Right now I just want to know what it—and you—have to do with Timmy's bedroom."

Jan sobered. "That's a long story too, Cherry. Oh, I forgot to ask you—may I call you Cherry? Timmy does."

"Almost everyone does soon after they meet me," Cherry admitted.

Jan's lovely face was now as bright as a summer sky after a sudden shower. "I like you, Cherry," she said. "I liked you the minute we first bumped into each other. I'm sorry you don't—well, approve of me." She went on in a rush of words, and completely won Cherry's heart. "I'm not really a cold-blooded thief. Honest, I'm not. And as for Mother, she really is a hypochondriac. Her own doctor told me so. She *works* herself up into those headaches. She hypnotizes herself into having pain. She does it whenever she can't have her own way. I've known it ever since I was a child. If Daddy wanted to go to the seashore and she wanted to go to the mountains, she'd have an attack. So we'd go to the mountains. Daddy let her get by with it, but I *won't!* She has no right to ruin my life. I don't want to make my debut next winter. I want to go to college. It takes years and years to become a good artist. I can't afford to waste one year going to silly parties, dancing with silly men, and selling tickets to silly charity balls."

"How old are you, Jan?" Cherry asked quietly.

"I was sixteen last month."

"So you'll be not quite seventeen if you go to college next fall," Cherry said mildly. "That's pretty young for college. The average age of a freshman is eighteen. Seems to me you could compromise with your mother. If she has her heart set on your having a debutante winter, why not give her a year of your life? After all, she *is* your mother. Even the most selfish mother makes plenty of sacrifices for her children. Few of us ever have a chance to repay our parents; this is your chance. I know I sound preachy, but you don't want to leave something undone which you may regret when it's too late to do anything about it."

Jan hung her head. "When you put it that way, it makes sense. And I do love Mother. But even if I do give in and 'come out' at a big ball next winter, she won't let me go to college the following year. Daddy left every single cent to her. I won't inherit a penny when I'm eighteen. I'll be dependent on her all the rest of my life." She shuddered violently. "I'm desperate, Cherry. I begged and begged her to at least let me take a business course at school, but she promptly had an attack. So all I can do is speak French and Spanish, fence, and recite Shakespeare. How can I support myself with nothing but a finishing school background?"

Cherry was beginning to understand the despair of this lovely young girl. She had a drive that must be given expression. Her mother was blindly selfish not to see it. Cherry said:

"I can sympathize with your desire for a career. I wanted dreadfully to become a nurse. I guess I was lucky having a family that encouraged me."

"You are lucky," Jan told her. "Nobody understands me. My aunts all say, 'Don't be silly, child. You'll be married before you're eighteen. It would be a waste of time and money to start in college.' But," she finished, "Uncle Benedict understood me. Oh, Cherry, he was the most wonderful old man! None of the other members of the family had anything to do with him. Because he was sort of an adventurer, you see. As salty as the sea, with the most marvelous sense of humor. He didn't mind being snubbed at all. Said his brothers and sisters were a bunch of stuffed shirts. And they are."

"Was he the Uncle Ben who told you about ambergris?" Cherry put in.

Jan nodded. "He not only told me about it, he *gave* it to me. But then he died, and now nobody knows where it is. I've got to find it. It must be somewhere in that stateroom."

Cherry's mouth fell open in surprise. "In Timmy's stateroom? Why on earth would it be there?"

Jan sighed. "I guess I had better begin at the beginning. It happened a few days before Thanksgiving when I was all alone in the apartment. Mother had gone to the theater and the servants had the afternoon off. The doorman called up from downstairs and said there was a 'peculiar character' calling to see Mother. Claimed to be her brother-in-law." Jan grinned. "That made him my uncle. I was downright curious to see an uncle whom William described as a 'peculiar character.' So I said, 'Send him right up, William.'

"I opened the door and there stood this big, raw-boned man with the most weather-beaten face you ever saw. He was wearing a rough coat that hadn't been pressed in years and a thick navy-blue sweater and tight, blue serge pants, and, believe it or not, Cherry, knee boots! No hat, and there was melting snow in his bushy white hair, and his hands were rough and red. I wouldn't have believed he was Daddy's 'black sheep' older brother, except for his eyes. They were my grandfather's own green, twinkling eyes. Granddaddy was a country banker. And although he was very rich, he drove around in a battered old Ford, and never put on airs. Everyone loved him."

"He sounds like a wonderful person," Cherry said.

"He was. And Uncle Benedict was an awful lot like him. His eyes twinkled at me and he said, 'You must be my niece, Jan. Never would have thought Rob and Nellie could produce such a beauty.' " Jan blushed. "I liked him right off. Not so much for the compliment as for the way he said it. Completely outspoken and frank in a deep, hearty voice. My other uncles flatter me in such a namby-pamby way I hate it. Well, anyway, Uncle Ben and I got on together from the very beginning. In less than an hour I was weeping on his shoulder about wanting to be an artist and how Mother wouldn't let me. He didn't say anything that day, but I saw a lot of him after that. Mother didn't approve, but I went ahead and met him away from home. We went for long walks through Central Park, and rode on the top of open buses even in bitter cold weather. And he told me about his different experiences and scrapes. Then one day he got to talking about ambergris. Said that it didn't smell awful at all but had the most delicate, exotic fragrance with a nice seaweedy smell too."

Jan leaned forward excitedly. "Uncle Ben said that during all the years that he roamed the seven seas he was always on the lookout for ambergris. Then one day when he and a pal were wandering along a beach in the Persian Gulf, they found a chunk of it. The most perfect type of fossil ambergris, or, as it's called, *ambre blanc,* because it's white. It had been lying there on the shore for centuries, perhaps. They knew from its texture and fine odor that it was not Fool's Gold this time. So they divided the lump into two equal parts, and came right back to America to sell it."

Cherry was so fascinated by this romantic tale that she forgot momentarily that she was a cruise nurse. "Go on," she urged Jan as the tall young girl got up and began to pace nervously up and down the room.

CHAPTER X

Jan's Problem

JAN CAME TO REST BESIDE CHERRY'S CHAIR. "WHEN Uncle Ben told me he'd actually found some priceless ambergris, naturally I was dying to see it. But he wouldn't show it to me then."

"Oh," Cherry put in. "Then he didn't sell it when he came back to America?"

Jan shook her head. "No, his pal sold his share in New York for about five thousand dollars and began to live like a king. Uncle Ben said his partner was much younger than he. Young enough to be his son. Uncle Ben was in his seventies, but the two of them had been traveling around together for years and years."

"Why didn't your uncle sell his share in New York?" Cherry wanted to know.

"I'm coming to that," replied Jan. "Uncle Ben suddenly got the notion that he'd like to settle down. He felt as young as ever, but for some reason he began to think about taking root somewhere. Ages ago, he had bought some property in Curaçao, but he left the running of it to his lawyer in Willemstad, the capital city. Squatters have been living rent free in the lovely old Dutch mansion at Piscadera Bay. So I imagine everything has been allowed to go to rack and ruin. Uncle made up his mind to use the money he got from his ambergris to fix the property up. He said it wouldn't take much to make it salable. Then, at the height of the tourist season, he would sell it for a fancy sum. It would make a swell site for a club or inn, he said."

"I can imagine that," Cherry said. "But how do you fit into the picture?"

Jan began to pace again. "After Uncle Ben sold the property, he was going to buy himself a smaller place on the island. The rest of the money he was going to give to me so I could go ahead and become an artist. He was awfully mad when he heard that Daddy had left everything to Mother. Daddy inherited from my grandfather, and Uncle Ben felt I should have been the sole heir. He himself was disinherited when he ran away from home as a boy. He didn't mind that at all. But he got so worked up about me he made out a will at once making me his sole heir, and sent it to his lawyer in Willemstad."

Jan smiled. "He was an old darling, Cherry. Eccentric as anything. No matter how much money he made throughout his checkered career, he never once had a bank account. Didn't believe in them. He had an old-fashioned money belt which he kept on him day and night. And yet for all of that, he wouldn't do a thing without first consulting his lawyer down in Willemstad. He wouldn't even sell his ambergris until Mr. Camelot said the price he was offered was right."

"Did he ever show you the ambergris?" Cherry asked.

Jan shook her head. "No, although I found out later that he had it with him whenever we went for those walks and bus rides. Finally one day he let me smell a pinch of it. It has the most delicate, out-of-this-world aroma, Cherry; like nothing else I ever knew. Then just about two weeks ago, Uncle Ben kissed me good-bye and sailed away on this very same ship to Curaçao. The next thing I knew he was dead." Jan tensely rubbed her eyes. "Mr. Camelot sent me a cable saying my uncle had been stricken at sea with pulmonary thrombosis and had died without regaining consciousness shortly after being taken ashore at Willemstad."

Cherry sat up straight. "Pulmonary thrombosis!" Jan's uncle, then, must have been the passenger so many people had mentioned during the past few days!

"The cable," Jan continued, "said that my entire in-heritance, besides a few hundred dollars Uncle Ben had carried with him, was the property at Piscadera Bay. In its present state of disrepair, Mr. Camelot im-plied, it was practically worthless. The cable ended by requesting me to state my wishes as to the disposition of the property."

"But the ambergris?" Cherry cried. "What happened to it?"

"That's the point," Jan cried. "What *did* happen to it? I cabled Mr. Camelot at once asking him if there wasn't something else of value in my uncle's luggage. The answer was no. Nothing, except what was in his money belt. Three hundred dollars and forty-nine cents, to be exact. Mr. Camelot, I suppose, thinking I didn't trust him, went so far as to list by cable collect the contents of my uncle's one and only suitcase which the steamship line sent ashore with him."

"What were the contents?" Cherry demanded. "Maybe the ambergris was hidden in a shoe."

Jan grinned ruefully. "No shoes. Boots, remember? And Uncle Ben virtually died with his boots on, just as he would have wanted to. The attack came on as the *Julita* was waiting for the pontoon bridge at Willemstad to open. Mr. Camelot came aboard the minute the ship docked and took Uncle Ben straight to a hospital. Uncle Ben believed in traveling light, I guess. In his suitcase were nothing but an extra sweater, socks, shirts, and pajamas."

"There must have been something else," Cherry argued. "Slippers, a comb, military brushes—you know, the things men always pack in their grips. Razor and toothbrush, certainly."

Jan shrugged. "I suppose all that sort of thing was in the suitcase too. But Mr. Camelot didn't bother to list them, thank goodness, since he was cabling collect. Mother was very stuffy about paying for those cables, I can tell you. And she refused at first when I insisted upon taking this trip. But when she found out that some of the 'best families' were taking the cruise, she was all for it. She doesn't know about Uncle Ben's ambergris. But don't you see, Cherry? The ambergris *must be still aboard this ship!*"

Cherry thought for a minute, and then nodded. "Somehow in the last-minute rush and the excitement of taking a dying passenger ashore, it wasn't packed with the other things."

"That's what I think," Jan said slowly. "In fact, I'm *sure* of it. So sure, that I went right down to the steamship line and tried to reserve the same room. I put on a big scene, cried like anything, insisting that for sentimental reasons I must have the same room in which my uncle had spoken his last words." She sighed. "They were very nice and understanding about it, but no go. It seems that 141 and 143 are almost always sold as suites. Last trip they did split the two rooms, but they don't like to. And the suite had already been reserved by a Mrs. Crane for this trip. The best they could do was to arrange things so we would be seated at the same table. Then I might be invited to visit in the room where my uncle practically breathed his last."

She whirled on Cherry stormily. "I know I sound awfully hard-boiled about this, but Uncle Ben wouldn't have wanted me to grieve. He had a wonderful, full life, and although he claimed he wanted to take root somewhere, I think he knew he was nearing the end of his journey. He told me himself that when he went, he wanted to go quickly. He had never been a grasping person, and he didn't intend to grasp at life." Jan was crying now. "'Honey,' he said, 'I've seen everything there is to see on this old globe. I'm tired. But I'm going to die with my boots on. You'll see.'"

Cherry said comfortingly: "He must have been a wonderful old gentleman. The surgeon and the purser both said he was a most unusual person."

"He *was* a gentleman," Jan said tautly. "He didn't have the manners and social graces my other uncles have. They're nice enough, I suppose, but Uncle Benedict was a man, Cherry. You couldn't help admiring and respecting his independence. He lived the way he wanted to without hurting anybody. And for all that he disinherited him, I think Benedict was my grandfather's favorite. They were very much alike."

Cherry stood up. It was almost four o'clock. "I've got to go now. But let me brood about it all for a little while. I can assure you right now, Jan, you have nothing to worry about. The ambergris is perfectly safe. Steamship lines are very careful about passengers' property. If it wasn't sent ashore with the other things in your uncle's cabin, it's in good hands. Probably at the home office in New York."

Jan shook her head. "I don't think so. They would have told me about it when I reserved our suite. Furthermore, this ship was completely modernized recently. There may be all sorts of recesses that were sealed up when it was redecorated. It would be just like Uncle Ben to find a secret panel and hide his ambergris behind it."

Cherry laughed. "I think you're letting your imagination run away witih you. But, with Timmy's permission, we'll both search his cabin carefully when I have plenty of time. No more secret searches. Promise?"

Jan hesitated, then held out her hand. "All right, Cherry. But we've got to work fast. Someone else is trying to find that ambergris. If he gets it first, that's that. I have no way of proving that it belongs to me."

Cherry looked puzzled. "Someone else? What do you mean?"

"The man Timmy calls Henry Morgan because he looks like a pirate," Jan said in a lowered voice. "Timmy himself told me his friend 'Henry' searched the top of the closet and took all of the toys out of the bottom storage space."

Cherry gasped. Mr. Rough Diamond! But that was ridiculous. How could anyone but Jan even guess that priceless ambergris had once been hidden in Timmy's room?

Jan, reading her thoughts, said quietly, "He *does* look like a pirate too. A seafaring man, anyway. Maybe Uncle Ben met him sometime or other in his wanderings, and told him he'd found some ambergris. He may have been following Uncle ever since, waiting for a chance to steal it. My very conventional relatives ran only the bare facts of Uncle Ben's death in the obituary columns for three days. But some reporter dug up the story of Uncle Ben's past and ran a front-page story about his being a very colorful member of our conservative family." Jan shrugged. "In the write-up, the reporter stated that Mr. Benedict Paulding died penniless except for some almost worthless property in the Netherlands West Indies. It made a nice anticlimax to the story of a soldier of fortune, and he played it up for all it was worth."

"But—" Cherry began. Jan interrupted:

"If Timmy's pirate had been on my uncle's trail he would have known that he had not yet sold the ambergris when he came aboard the *Julita*. Since it was not in his possession at the time of his death, it must be still on the ship. Even *I* figured that out, and our Mr. Henry Morgan, from the one glimpse I had of him, is a lot shrewder than I am."

Cherry smiled. "Well, you're not exactly stupid, Jan. At first I thought you were very young for your age, but now I think exactly the opposite. In some ways, you're a very mature young lady." She held out her hand. "Let's find that ambergris and make sure you can go to college. *After* you've made your mother happy by playing social butterfly for a few months."

Jan grinned as she shook Cherry's hand gratefully. "You win about that angle of it. I can take art lessons in between parties. But we've got to act fast. I haven't a cent for the taxes on that property at Piscadera Bay."

Cherry nodded and then she peeked into the other room to make sure Mrs. Paulding was still sleeping peacefully.

As she hurried down to sick bay, she thought: "Mr. Henry-Morgan-Rough-Diamond will bear watching."

She made a mental note never to afford him another opportunity to be alone with Timmy in Stateroom 141. But she formed this resolution too late. When she came up to take Timmy's T.P.R. a few minutes later, she found Mr. Rough Diamond himself, sitting on the foot of Timmy's bed!

CHAPTER XI

Timmy's Pirate

TIMMY TOOK HIS WORSHIPFUL EYES AWAY FROM HIS pirate long enough to glare at Cherry:

"Go 'way. Can't you see Henry is telling me a story?"

"Henry" arose to his feet in one smooth, graceful motion. "So we meet again, Miss Cherry? May I introduce myself? I am Henry Landgraf. Your little patient guessed my first name correctly."

Cherry reluctantly held out a limp hand. There was nothing else to do. She had not one bit of evidence to prove her suspicions. Even though she was positive Mr. Henry Landgraf had ransacked Timmy's cabin, she could expect no help from the little boy. He obviously adored this big, sunburnt man and would defend him with might and main.

Cherry pulled herself together and donned her most professional manner. "It was very kind of you to amuse

123

my patient in my absence. Now I must ask you to leave. It is time for his inhalation."

Tim promptly kicked off the covers and began to bounce up and down in rage. "If Henry goes away, I won't breathe inside that old tent of yours. I'll shut my mouth and hold my nose."

Mr. Landgraf slid admiring eyes from Cherry to the little boy on the bed. "Timothy Crane," he said in a gruff growl, "if you want to be a pirate you must learn to take orders. You do exactly what Miss Cherry says or I'll make you walk the plank at sundown."

Timmy howled with laughter, relishing the thought of such an unusual and bloodcurdling punishment. He grabbed the umbrella and waved it, cutlass fashion. Then he snatched up an empty pop bottle and twirled it expertly, chanting:

> *"Fifteen men on the dead man's chest—*
> *Yo-ho-ho and a bottle of rum!"*

"One thing you can say in my favor, Miss Cherry," Mr. Landgraf said humbly. "Tim and I have collected quite a lot of bottle tops during this session."

"They're not bottle tops!" Timmy explained. "They're pieces of eight. Pieces of eight!" He reached under his bunk and produced an empty candy box that had been painted to resemble a treasure chest.

Cherry saw with satisfaction that it contained quite a respectable quantity of "pieces of eight." She couldn't help smiling her approval at the tall "pirate."

He bowed and moved in that graceful swagger of his to the door. "If you have any trouble with Captain Kidd, don't hesitate to call on me."

"Thank you," Cherry murmured primly, "but I don't anticipate any difficulty. He is a very good patient."

Amusement flickered in the bright blue eyes. "Perhaps. But for your information I found him out in the corridor not long ago practicing handsprings. I'm no tattletale, but I know laryngitis when I *hear* it."

There was just a hint of implied criticism in his deep voice. Cherry's cheeks flamed.

"I don't believe it. I left the child with his mother. She wouldn't leave him alone."

The heavy shoulders shrugged. "Nevertheless, apparently she did. She's down at the pool right now. Or was, half an hour ago."

Cherry bit her lip. How could Mrs. Crane have done such a thing? It just wasn't possible. She must have turned Timmy over to a maid or stewardess who was suddenly called away.

Cherry was almost afraid to take Timmy's temperature. But in spite of his exciting afternoon, it was right on the dot of normal. Cherry breathed a sigh of relief. As she spooned his medication into him, Timmy rambled on about his new-found friend.

"Henry," he told her, "is an awful smart man. 'Most as smart as my daddy. But *he* can't find Fuzzy-Wuzzy either. We played 'cold and hot,' you know, and I kept telling him he was *freezing* when he tapped the walls and looked in the back of all the bureau drawers. Guess nobody will ever find Fuzzy-Wuzzy but *me*."

So, between tales of piracy on the high seas, Mr. Landgraf had got in a bit of searching. Probably he had been able to get in *quite* a bit of searching.

When the inhalation was over, Mrs. Crane came back, sunburnt and happy as a lark. Cherry decided to risk a rebuff, if not a complaint to the captain.

"Mrs. Crane," she said sternly, "I don't believe you quite understand about Timmy. He must not be left alone. Under no circumstances must he be allowed out of bed. While you were down at the pool another passenger found him playing in the corridor."

Mrs. Crane's pink face turned red. "But he was sound asleep, Miss Ames," she defended herself. "At home he generally naps for an hour or more. I didn't leave until three-thirty and I knew you'd look in at four."

Cherry lost her temper then. She said a lot of things she knew she had no business saying. "I simply can't understand your attitude, Mrs. Crane." Doggedly she followed her into the living room and closed the door. "You don't seem to appreciate the fact that you have an exceptionally bright little boy. A sick little boy. A half-starved little boy."

Mrs. Crane tossed her pretty head. "It's not my fault he won't eat. They sent up spinach and liver. He detests them both."

Cherry went on ruthlessly. "I'm not talking about spinach and liver. I'm talking about mother love."

Mrs. Crane flounced to the French windows and stared out on deck. "Nanny adores him. She's been with him ever since we came home from the hospital. He worships the ground she walks on." She whirled around to face Cherry defiantly. "If you want to know the truth, Miss Ames, I'd like to win Timmy away from Nanny. That's why I took him on this cruise. But it hasn't worked out at all. I thought we would spend all our time around the pool. We'd have fun together." She began to sob with self-pity. "I was going to teach him to swim and turn somersaults in the water. We'd get to know each other that way, and then he'd learn to love me."

Cherry felt a twinge of pity. She said more gently:

"The cruise has hardly begun. Timmy's temperature was normal at four. If it stays that way we'll take him off sulfa in another twenty-four hours. Then we can take him out on deck for sun baths. In another day or so he'll be up and around. You'll have plenty of time for fun with him at the pool."

Mrs. Crane sniffled. "I know you think I'm a perfect moron, but really the whole blame rests on my mother-in-law's shoulders. I wanted to take care of Timmy as a baby, but she wouldn't hear of it. We live with her, you see. I wish we didn't. My husband is her only child. She arranges both of our lives to suit herself. Mine is just one social engagement after another. I hardly ever see Timmy."

"Well, I certainly would change all that when you get home," Cherry said firmly. "You can, you know. Your husband will back you up. In the meantime, you can start getting rid of Nanny by convincing Timmy that you can take better care of him than she can. I'll teach you how to give him a bed bath, and how to change the sheets without moving him. He'll love that."

"Oh, would you, really?" Mrs. Crane was pathetically grateful. "Do you think I could learn? I'm so utterly helpless."

Cherry chuckled. "You just think you are. Hundreds of so-called helpless society women work in hospitals as nurses' aides. We couldn't get along without them."

Timmy yelled impatiently then. Cherry hurried to him, hoping that at least she had impressed on his mother that he must not be left alone again. A docile Mrs. Crane followed on Cherry's heels.

Timmy was demanding a toy parrot. He had seen one in the shop on A deck. "I'm Long John Silver," he shouted. "I *have* to have a parrot. Pieces of eight. Pieces of eight." He let a handful of bottle tops cascade through his fat fingers. "Pieces of eight!"

"I'll get you a parrot right away, honey." Mrs. Crane snatched up her handbag and darted out into the corridor. She was in such a hurry she barely escaped colliding with Dr. Monroe who had just raised his knuckles to knock.

"Hello, Tim," he said. "Has Cherry been taking good care of you?"

Timmy proudly pointed to his collection of bottle tops. "When are we going to play checkers?"

Dr. Monroe glanced inquiringly at Cherry.

"Perfectly normal," she said. "And he's not nearly so hoarse as he was."

The ship's surgeon nodded. He strode across the room and flung open the French doors. "Let's get a little of that good warm air in here. If it's fair tomorrow and his temperature is still normal, we'll wheel him out on deck. How about it, Tim?"

Timmy grinned. "Also, I've got to go swimming soon. I've *got* to. For a very 'portant reason."

Cherry told Dr. Monroe, "He's been a pirate all day, you see."

The word "pirate" started Timmy off again. Dr. Monroe had to listen to a very Timmy-version of how the pirates divided the booty among themselves. He was very proud of one fact which he explained clearly. Before the loot was apportioned into shares, certain payments were always taken out. One of the first payments was for medical care.

"Those buccaneers," Timmy chuckled gleefully. "They were always losing a hand or a leg or an eye. Henry's going to make me a patch so I can pe-tend I've only got one eye."

Dr. Monroe joined in Cherry's laughter. "He's got the makings of a good surgeon, hasn't he? Nothing squeamish about Tim Crane."

"I should say not," Cherry agreed. "He'll never go back to Mother Goose after this trip. Anything else but the stories in your book will be too tame for him now."

Mrs. Crane came back with the bright-feathered toy parrot then. Cherry and the doctor left, almost deafened by cries of "Pieces of eight! Pieces of eight!"

"He's a cute kid," Kirk Monroe said as they walked down toward the Paulding suite.

Cherry, though hating herself for it, had to report Timmy's activity in the corridor to the young surgeon.

Dr. Monroe shook his head. "I don't like to say this, Cherry, but I'm afraid I'm going to have to ask you to sleep in Timmy's room tonight. I'm afraid his mother might not wake up and give him his midnight and four o'clock doses of sulfa. It'll be much less of a chore for you if you're sleeping in the other twin bed. Mrs. Crane can have the sofa-bed in the living room made up for herself."

"I don't mind at all, Dr. Monroe," Cherry said.

He stopped outside Stateroom 125. "Oh, let's cut out this doctor and nurse stuff. We're on a pleasure cruise; let's get some fun out of it." He grinned boyishly. "Unless you object, I'd like you to call me Kirk. We were both on duty in the Pacific so that makes us old friends, doesn't it?"

Cherry said happily, "Yes, doctor! *Kirk!*" She knew, of course, that it would still be "Doctor" and "Nurse" when they made professional calls on patients. But in-between times it would be Cherry and Kirk. Thank goodness. The ship's surgeon must like her, must think they were making a good team.

~~~~~~

CHAPTER XII

Caught Off Bounds!

WHEN THEY KNOCKED ON THE DOOR OF STATEROOM 125, Jan opened it. She looked relieved at the sight of the doctor and his nurse.

"Oh, I'm so glad you came. Mother's awake," she whispered. "And, oh, so cross. She always is after she's had morphine."

Mrs. Paulding called out fretfully from her bed, "Is that you, Doctor?"

Kirk Monroe, with Cherry at his side, strode into the room. "Good afternoon, Mrs. Paulding. Are you feeling better?"

Mrs. Paulding screwed her fat, pasty face into a frown. "I feel simply ghastly," she moaned. "I shouldn't have let you give me that morphine. I'm allergic to it. My system just won't tolerate it."

Kirk's cool fingers were on her wrist. He smiled briefly. "I think it would do you good to get out of bed

131

and perhaps sit out on deck for a while. You are no longer suffering any pain, are you, Mrs. Paulding?"

She pursed her pale lips into a pout. "I'm not in *pain,* but I am certainly far too weak to promenade the deck. I don't know how you can suggest such a thing!"

Kirk nodded coldly. "You know best. We'll look in on you again this evening."

He turned and walked into the other room with Cherry and Jan right on his heels. Jan closed the living-room door:

"Well, Doctor?" she demanded. "Mother's not really sick, is she?"

Kirk shrugged. "Not being her private physician I wouldn't want to make such a definite statement. However, I will go so far as to say I believe there is a psychological factor in the frequency of her headaches. I imagine they often follow emotional upsets. Right?"

"Right. Oh, so right," Jan said. "This last attack, for instance, was brought on because I refused to go swimming with a young man we met in the club at tea yesterday."

Kirk's eyebrows shot up in amusement. "Why wouldn't you go swimming with him?"

"Simply because Mother wanted me to," Jan said flatly.

Kirk laughed outright then. "You remind me of a little boy we had in the children's ward when I was an intern. The only way we could get him to eat his oatmeal was to stand around his crib and forbid him to take a mouthful."

Cherry giggled, and finally Jan relaxed into a sheepish grin. "I know I'm silly. I should give in to Mother on the simple things and save my strength for times when it's really important."

"It's worth trying," Cherry said emphatically. She added to Kirk: "Jan's a very intelligent young woman—*except* in her relationship with her mother."

Cherry and Dr. Monroe said good-bye to Jan. "You're a real nurse," he said, smiling. "And you certainly have a way with people. Tim adores you. And as for Bill, you're his pin-up girl. You should see the portrait he's sketching of you. Glamour plus, Cherry. To pun—a left-handed compliment."

Cherry blushed. "What about Bill? He's getting awfully bored in sick bay."

"That's right," Kirk agreed. "I'm sending him back to his own quarters tonight. After Christmas he can be given easy jobs, although he'll wear the cast for several weeks."

"Then after his eight-o'clock checkup I can consider him as discharged?"

"I'll check him at eight myself," Kirk said. "And then discharge him from sick bay. You'll be busy with Timmy anyway. Sure you don't mind bunking in his room tonight? It doesn't exactly come under the heading of one of your duties, you know."

"It'll be fun," Cherry said. "He's a lamb."

Dr. Monroe glanced at his watch. "We may as well have dinner now. It's almost time. If we go early we can get a table together."

Dinner was a pleasant interlude in Cherry's busy day. It was "Kirk" and "Cherry" from the crab-meat cocktails right down through lobster Newburg and cheese and crackers.

Brownie, from the table behind Kirk's back, went through all sorts of motions signifying jealousy and a broken heart. Cherry could hardly keep a straight face.

After dinner she went to her cabin and packed a little overnight kit. Timmy was ecstatic when he heard Cherry was going to sleep in the other twin bed.

"We'll play guessing games all night long," he announced. *"First!"*

"All right," Cherry said as she plugged in the vaporizer kettle. "You go first."

Wriggling, but speaking slowly and carefully, as though he had just learned the question by heart, Timmy asked:

"Why did the pirate bring his cutlass and pistol to the corner?"

"I give up," Cherry said after a moment. "Why?"

"Cause he didn't know whether to cut across the street or shoot down the alley!" Timmy announced triumphantly.

Cherry laughed and came back with: "Why did the moron go to the zoo on the night before Christmas?"

"That's too easy," Timmy chortled. "To buy some Christmas seals, 'course!"

Mrs. Crane came in then and watched interestedly while Cherry gave Tim a bed bath and changed the sheets.

"It looks so easy when you do it," she admitted. "But I will try tomorrow if you'll let me."

Timmy looked up, wide-eyed. "Is Mummy going to give me a bath?"

Cherry nodded. "She certainly is. And she's going to rub your back with some nice, sweet-smelling powder too. Then, if it's a nice day, she's going to help you get dressed and take you out on deck for a while."

Timmy looked doubtful. "Can *she* tie shoelaces?"

"Of course," Cherry assured him.

"That's good," Timmy said, relieved. "Cause Nanny can't. They always come undone."

"Your mummy," Cherry went on quickly, "will teach you how to tie your own shoelaces so they won't come undone any more."

"I'll show you how to tie them in double knots the way my mother showed me, Timmy," Mrs. Crane said bravely.

Timmy went off on another tangent. "Henry's going to show me how to tie a bowline. That's the kind of knot you use when you want to hang somebody from the mast." He grinned impishly up at Cherry as Mrs. Crane hurried away to dinner. "Say, Cherry, did you hear about the sailor who climbed the fifty-foot mast and fell bang! down on the deck?"

"Oh, my goodness," Cherry gasped. "How awful. The poor man!"

"Poor man nothin'," Timmy sniffed. "He didn't even get hurt."

"Timmy Crane," Cherry said. "You're fibbing."

Timmy bounced in glee. "'Course he didn't get hurt, silly. He only climbed up two feet."

"Who's been telling you all these jokes, Tim?" Cherry asked suspiciously.

"Henry," Timmy said. "He's still looking for my Fuzzy-Wuzzy, you know. He came knocking on the door while you were gone, pe-tending he came to see Mummy. But course he really came to see me. *Also,* Mummy told him she wanted to see how Jan's mummy was feeling so Henry said he'd play games with me until she came back. *Also,* he didn't find Fuzzy-Wuzzy," he finished, exulting.

As Cherry took Timmy's temperature she said quietly, "May Jan and I look for Fuzzy-Wuzzy sometime too?"

"Jan," Tim said in disgust. "She couldn't find *any*-thing. But you can play, Cherry."

Cherry saw that his temperature had gone up, as was to be expected at that hour, to 101°. "What is Fuzzy-Wuzzy, anyway?" she asked, mildly curious. "Another duck?"

"Duck?" Tim fell back on the pillows. "Course not! He's my black-and-white bear. Nanny says he's a panda, but *I* know he's a bear."

"Didn't you ever see the pandas at the zoo, Timmy?" Cherry asked.

"Sure. But they're bears too."

Cherry corrected him gently. "They're not, Timmy. They don't even belong to the bear family."

"So what?" Timmy said airily. "I asked Granny to give me a Teddy bear for my birthday. And she gave me Fuzzy-Wuzzy. So I pe-tend he's a bear."

Cherry wondered about Granny, pretty little Mrs. Crane's mother-in-law. Why couldn't she have given the child what he asked for? Cherry shrugged. Probably because she considered a panda more modern. Would the domineering grandmother try to run Timmy's life too? Cherry hoped not. There was still time for young Mrs. Crane to take matters in her own hands.

"Once she's put in entire charge of Timmy's care," Cherry decided, "she'll never turn him over to Nanny again. Gradually, I've got to make her assume the responsibility herself."

Cherry, after her sleepless night during the storm, was glad to undress and go to bed as soon as Timmy had had his medication and inhalation.

They played guessing games until they both fell asleep simultaneously in the middle of a question. Cherry had set her alarm for 11:45, but she awoke with a start at ten.

Timmy was quietly sobbing in the other bed: "I want my Fuzzy-Wuzzy. I want my Fuzzy-Wuzzy."

Cherry scrambled to his bed and took him in her arms. He was half awake, half dreaming. She said comfortingly: "I'll get him for you, honey. Tell me where you hid him."

But he only kept on sobbing: "I want my Fuzzy-Wuzzy. I *have* to have my Fuzzy-Wuzzy."

Cherry searched every nook and cranny in the cabin. There was no sign of a little black-and-white panda. Timmy would not stop crying. Cherry looked into the other room and saw that Mrs. Crane had not yet returned from dinner. She was no doubt dancing in the club, taking advantage of Cherry in the capacity of both nurse and "sitter."

Timmy began to punctuate his sobs with sharp, racking coughs. That would never do.

Gently, Cherry shook him until he was more fully awake. "I can't find your Fuzzy-Wuzzy," she said. "You must tell me where you hid him. Then I'll get him for you right away."

Timmy looked doubtful. "Promise?"

"Promise."

"Cross your heart and hope to die?"

"Cross my heart and hope to die."

Timmy's shoulders stopped shaking immediately. "He's in the swimming pool," he said.

Cherry gasped. "In the pool? How on earth did he get there?"

"I dropped him," Timmy said. "Early this morning while Mummy was still asleep, I went out to see that pool. And Fuzzy-Wuzzy said he wanted to go swimming. So I let him go."

"Oh, Timmy," Cherry moaned. "Did he sink right away?"

"Not *right* away," Timmy told her. "He floated around looking up at me. And then I couldn't see him any more. He went under the diving board."

The little panda must be at the bottom of the pool now, in the shadow of the diving board. That was why nobody had seen him and returned him to Timmy. There were no other children aboard ship.

"I'm sorry, Timmy, I can't get him for you," Cherry said desperately. "I'm not allowed to go in the pool."

Timmy's face flamed. "You promised," he shouted in uncontrollable rage. *"You promised!"*

"I know I did," Cherry admitted regretfully. "But I thought Fuzzy-Wuzzy was in your room somewhere."

"You *knew* he wasn't," Timmy howled, "I *tole* you so. I told you Henry was *freezing* when he looked around in here."

"Oh, dear," Cherry sighed inwardly. "How can I ever make this little boy understand rules and regulations? He'll think I just don't want to keep my promise. He won't trust me any more and I'll never be able to do another thing with him."

Timmy's tirade made it all too clear that Cherry, if she refused to keep her promise, was "out" as far as Timmy was concerned. "I won't stay inside my tent," he yelled. "I won't eat anything. I won't drink anything. I won't stay covered up, I'll jump overboard and get all drownded. Then you'll be sorry!"

He screamed on and on, between spasms of coughing.

Cherry said as calmly as possible: "I'll ring for a steward, Timmy. Waidy will get your bear for you."

"Don't want Waidy to get him. Want *you* to get him. You promised."

"Waidy will get your mother, Timmy," Cherry said, without much hope. "She'll bring you back Fuzzy-Wuzzy."

"No, she won't!" Timmy kicked off the covers and straggled to get out of bed. "I tole her to get him this morning. She's an ole 'fraidy-cat. Scared to go in deep water."

Cherry gave up. After all, what harm was there in her taking a quick dip in the pool? It was a silly restriction anyway, as Ziggy had pointed out: "As though you and Doc, the cleanest people aboard ship, might contaminate the water."

Doc! That reminded Cherry of Rule 7. "When in doubt the ship's nurse is always to consult the ship's surgeon."

But that meant disturbing Kirk's rest. He had had no sleep the night before either.

And Timmy was now in a dangerous state of excitement. She must act quickly. The chances were that none of the passengers would recognize her out of uniform. To most of them, she was nothing but an automaton in a stiffly starched white dress and cap. Charlie's Christmas present would be a perfect disguise.

"All right," she said to Timmy, tucking him back in bed. "I'll get your little bear. But you've got to keep covered while I'm gone."

Timmy's sobs immediately subsided. "I knew you would, Cherry." He grinned. "You're just like me. You *always* keep your promises. I won't get out of bed even if a big 'normous pirate comes in and chops off my head."

Cherry hugged him. "Nobody's going to chop off your head. Ill bring Fuzzy back just as soon as I can."

She raced down the corridor, leaving the door slightly ajar behind her, and her thoughts raced too. Perhaps the missing panda was the answer to the missing ambergris. Timmy himself might have found the precious powder in a box or a jar that very first day aboard ship. Like most little boys' favorite toys, Fuzzy could easily have burst open at the seam that joined its head to its body. And it would be just like Timmy to cram something in that opening.

If that were true, Jan's ambergris must now be at the bottom of the pool!

In her own cabin Cherry quickly changed from pajamas to the lovely rose taffeta suit. It took but a minute to slip into beach clogs, then with her soft terry cloth robe wrapped around her, she hurried up to the pool.

It was still crowded with passengers, and Cherry mingled with those who were chatting and laughing around the diving board. Nobody paid any attention to her at all.

She caught a glimpse of Jan and a nice looking boy leaning against the rail of the veranda above the pool. Oh, why hadn't she thought of Jan? Jan would have been delighted to help out. But it was too late now. It would take too long for Jan to change from that long flowered chiffon frock to a bathing suit.

Cherry didn't dare risk attracting attention by diving off the board. She slipped unobtrusively down the steps. The first dive was unsuccessful. On the second, she saw something dark on the bottom under the board. After the third she came up triumphantly with a very waterlogged little black and white panda. One squeeze told her that it was stuffed with nothing but wet cotton.

"Well," she thought, shaking herself, "I've christened Charlie's present anyway. So far so good. If I can only get back to my cabin without getting caught!"

Cherry had to admit that she had enjoyed her illegal dip in the cool, salty water of the tiled pool. Refreshed and glowing, she slipped into her robe and clogs. Now to stroll unconcernedly away.

She was halfway down the steps to B deck when she heard someone coming up. In another moment she saw that it was the steward, Waidler, bearing a tray of soft drinks.

Cherry sucked in her breath. Would he recognize her? If he did, he would most certainly report her to the captain. That meant dismissal. Dishonorable discharge, in other words.

Cherry was tempted to turn and flee back up the stairs. But that, of course, would only make matters worse. If she kept right on going as though she had every right in the world to be wandering around in a terry cloth robe at 10:30 P.M., he might not even give her a passing glance.

Gripping the soggy panda, she marched on, head held high. They passed each other on the landing. Out of the corner of her left eye Cherry noted with relief that apparently Waidler had not recognized her. But, a few steps above her, he stopped.

She could feel his eyes boring into her back. Her knees began to wobble, but somehow she managed to keep on going.

CHAPTER XIII

A Stolen Letter

IT WAS A HOT, ALMOST TROPICAL NIGHT, BUT CHERRY WAS shaking as though the ship were plying its way through Arctic icebergs.

Waidler, she felt sure, had recognized her. His attitude from the very beginning had been unfriendly, to say the least. Furthermore, Ziggy had told her that Waidler was a very conscientious steward. Even if he and Cherry were the best of friends, he might well feel that it was his duty to report her. She had flagrantly violated two rules:

"Out of uniform aboard ship." And, very obviously, "out of bounds."

He couldn't have missed her damply curling black hair. Waidler knew that Cherry had been in the pool!

Back in her own cabin, Cherry rubbed herself dry and donned pajamas and wrapper. The bunny-toed scuffs warmed her nervously icy feet. What would the next morning bring?

Dr. Monroe would not be "Kirk" when he reprimanded her. He would he very much the dignified young ship's surgeon. And the captain—the Old Man—? Would he put her ashore at Curaçao? Bleakly Cherry faced disgrace—the end of her nursing career.

And then, to cap the climax, when she hurried into Stateroom 141, she found Timmy fast asleep, one hand curled peacefully under his fat, rosy cheek.

For a moment Cherry felt like bursting into tears. She should have realized that Timmy couldn't possibly care very much about his panda. If he had, he would have demanded it a long time ago. He had simply put on a scene—just for the fun of it. And she had foolishly sacrificed her nurse's reputation to fulfill a childish whim.

"That's Ames for you," she told herself sternly. "Always letting the heart rule the head. Will you *ever* learn?"

But she had her reward when the alarm clock went off an hour later. Timmy's eyes popped open, and then, when he saw what was sitting damply on his glass-topped bed table, his eyes grew big as saucers.

"My Fuzzy-Wuzzy! My fuzzy little Fuzzy-Wuzzy. I thought you had drownded. But Cherry saved you, didn't she, Fuzzy?"

Cherry carefully pinned a square of rubber sheeting around the soggy little panda. Timmy cradled him in his arms, crooning:

"Nobody could find you, 'cept Cherry. Cherry's even smarter than Henry. I *tole* Henry you were on the bottom of the pool. But he just laughed and laughed. He didn't b'lieve me."

Cherry's heart went out to the little boy. He hadn't dared hope that he would ever see his panda again. That was why he hadn't asked for it. To Timmy, the pool must seem as bottomless as the ocean. The poor lamb had been silently yearning for his pet ever since he had watched Fuzzy float under the diving board.

Suddenly Cherry had a thought. She had already committed two crimes; why not another? All three of them were for the same good cause. She could hear Mrs. Crane coming into the next room now.

"I didn't save Fuzzy, Timmy," Cherry said in a clear voice. "Your mother did. When I got to the pool she had already found him. She's not a 'fraidy cat. She went right into the deep water and dived and dived until she came up with your little bear."

Mrs. Crane rustled into the bedroom. She looked puzzled, but Cherry silenced her with a quick glance.

Timmy held out his arms. "Mummy, *you* got my Fuzzy-Wuzzy! You're just 'bout the smartest person in the whole wide world."

Cherry left them hugging each other. In the bathroom she pounded the sulfa tablets to a powder. Then she mixed the medication with a jar of strained apricots. As she approached the bed, Timmy said firmly:

"I want my mummy to feed me."

Mrs. Crane smiled gratefully up at Cherry. Her lips said, "You darling, you!"

At the moment Cherry was glad she had told a deliberate lie. But the next morning she was not so sure. With Cherry supervising, Mrs. Crane had prepared Timmy's sulfa mixture, taken his temperature, which was normal, given him his inhalation, bathed and dressed him for breakfast.

"There," Cherry whispered when they were alone together in the bathroom. "It wasn't so bad, was it?"

"It was fun," Mrs. Crane admitted. "As long as the mercury stops at that nice red arrow I guess I can read his temperature all right."

Cherry turned to go back to Timmy and froze in her tracks. Waidler had just come in with the little boy's breakfast tray.

Cherry held her breath. Would he accuse her in front of passengers, or would he wait? Had he already reported her?

Waidler was staring, as though fascinated, at the little black and white panda. Timmy displayed his pet proudly:

"See, Waidy? Fuzzy didn't get drownded after all. My mummy went right into the deep, deep water and got him back for me."

The steward set down the tray and said gruffly, "Well, that's good, Tim."

He knew perfectly well that Mrs. Crane had not even appeared in a bathing suit the night before. She had been wearing a lovely full-skirted gown of crisp white pique, from dinnertime to midnight.

Waidler picked up the damp panda. "So this is the Fuzzy-Wuzzy you've been talking about all the time?"

"That's right," Timmy said. "I wanted him awful much cause he *always* sleeps with me. And last night when I couldn't sleep, my mummy got him for me."

Waidler left without giving Cherry so much as a glance. She thought agonizedly: "Now he despises me. He thinks I lied to protect myself. I could never convince him that I lied to Timmy for his mother's sake."

Cherry had not yet had breakfast, but somehow she couldn't bring herself to the point of going out into the rest of the ship and meeting her fate. But a cup of hot coffee might help to bring back her courage, and if she didn't go to the grill soon it would be too late.

She set her shoulders. Might as well go now and get it over with. Mrs. Crane had already started on the tea and toast Waidler had brought with Timmy's oatmeal and cocoa. She said:

"Run along, Cherry dear. And you don't need to come back till noon. Even then all you'll have to do is supervise. Without you watching me, I'd be sure to give him benzoin instead of sulfa."

Cherry got out a weak laugh, but she said encouragingly, "No, you wouldn't. You could really take over from now on, but I want an excuse to keep on seeing my favorite patient."

"Mummy and I are going to make a pirate ship," Timmy said, his mouth full. "The sheets are going to be sails and the 'brella is going to be the mast."

Out in the corridor Cherry sighed. "You've made a pretty mess of everything, Ames," she told herself grimly. But, somehow, she didn't regret any of it. Sometimes two wrongs did make a right. Timmy and his mother were very close to each other now; so close that Nanny didn't have a chance. And as for "Granny"—she had better abdicate in favor of young Mrs. Crane if she knew what was good for her.

Brownie, who was just finishing breakfast in the grill, beckoned to Cherry excitedly. "So scuttlebutt already has my own private scandal," Cherry thought. "And what a juicy tidbit it's going to be."

But Brownie had other gossip to impart. She seemed to have no idea that Cherry was in disgrace, on the verge of dismissal. She whispered:

"Have you heard the latest? The purser's office was broken into again last night! Miranda was just telling me that she heard nothing had been taken from the safe the first time, and this morning the only thing Ziggy could find missing in his office was the carbon copy of a completely unimportant letter. Somebody who knows something about safe combinations and locks is having himself a time, huh?"

Cherry managed to hide her surprise. "Probably a passenger with a warped sense of humor," she said easily.

"Probably," Brownie agreed. "By the way," she said suddenly, "where were you last night? I tapped on your door at nine and again at ten, but there was no answer. Miranda has a swell little portable victrola. We thought you might like to listen to some of the new records she got for Christmas presents."

Christmas! Why, today was Cherry's birthday. A fine Christmas Eve she was going to have! She took such a long time answering Brownie's question that the plump little stewardess said again, this time suspiciously:

"Well, where *were* you last night?"

Cherry came out of her mournful reverie. "With a patient," she said. "Little Timmy Crane. He's on sulfa, every four hours, day and night, you see."

"But that's not answering my question," Brownie went on, more suspicious than ever. "That's explaining where you were at eight, midnight and four this morning. But it isn't saying where you were at nine and ten last night."

"Oh, my goodness," Cherry thought, almost amused. "She thinks I'm the one who broke into Ziggy's office!" She said, smiling: "I spent the night in the Crane suite."

"Why, I never heard of such a thing," Brownie exploded. "It says right in the rules and regulations that except when her help is needed in the care of women passengers or women members of the crew, the nurse is not to have night duty."

"I know," Cherry said, suddenly weary of the whole talk. "Dr. Monroe did not order me to spend the night in Timmy's room. He requested it, and in the end it was easier for me to be right there. Don't you see?"

Brownie looked doubtful. She waited until Cherry had finished breakfast, then followed her down to her cabin. And there, damply hanging from a hook on the inside of her open closet door, was the rose taffeta bathing suit Brownie had admired on Friday. All too obviously, it had been christened recently.

Brownie stared at it and let out a long whistle. "So that's where you were last night, Cherry Ames. In the swimming pool!"

"That's right," Cherry said, not really caring much what Brownie thought any more. "I went in to get Timmy's panda which he'd dropped into the pool. Now, go and report me to the Old Man. Waidler knows I broke Rule Eleven, too. I guess everybody on the ship knows by now."

Brownie's mouth fell open. *"Me* report you? Are you crazy? I think it's wonderful you had the nerve to break that silly old rule. I guess you're not as stiff and starched as I thought you were." She grinned shamefacedly. "Just for a little while, though, I did kind of think you might have taken that letter from the purser's files. After all, you do have a key, you know."

"So I do," Cherry remembered, immediately forgiving Brownie for suspecting her. "But I'm not concerned with anything but the contents of the medical refrigerator."

To herself she added: "Or am I? I surely would like to have a look at the carbon copy of that 'completely unimportant' letter."

Brownie yawned. "Well, I'm off to my chores. But you'd better hide that damp little garment before one of the maids sees it."

She left before Cherry could remind her that Waidler already knew.

Cherry, feeling like a prisoner in the dock, waiting to be sentenced, sat on the edge of her bed. In spite of her own worries, her thoughts kept coming back to Jan and her problems.

The ambergris must be on board the *Julita*. But, Cherry felt sure, it was not in Timmy's cabin. She and Jan and Henry Landgraf had all searched Stateroom 141 thoroughly.

Apparently the fabulously valuable powder was not at the home office in New York. Neither was it in the purser's safe for, according to Jan, her uncle would never have put it in the safe. He would have kept it close beside him in his cabin, just as he wore his money belt day and night. But it was not in the money belt or the lawyer, Camelot, would have listed it in his cable to Jan.

Therefore, Cherry reasoned, it must have been accidentally left behind when the dying man was taken ashore. And then she remembered something Ziggy had *almost* said about Waidler that first day in sick bay.

"Efficient as all get out," Ziggy had said. "But even *he* slips up every now and then. Like at Willemstad last trip—."

Ziggy had clamped his mouth shut after that. So now Cherry was almost certain of what had happened. An elderly, blustering, salty old passenger whom Waidler couldn't get on with, stricken with pulmonary thrombosis just as the ship entered the port of Willemstad.

A dying passenger met at the dock by his lawyer and rushed ashore.

Waidler, cranky and upset by this unusual occurrence, flinging Uncle Ben's clothes into his suitcase. A hasty inventory of the shelves and drawers as the dying man was wheeled down the gangplank.

Then, later that Tuesday, *after* the ship had left Curaçao, Waidler, not so hurried now, would give the cabin one last inspection before the maids tore it apart for a thorough cleaning. Then, and not until then, would he discover that he had neglected to pack all of the eccentric old gentleman's effects.

What would he do with these items? Turn them over to the purser, of course. But then the purser would have placed them in a sealed container of some sort, listing the contents, and deposited these overlooked effects with the home office. He certainly would have done that sometime between Wednesday and Friday while the *Julita* was in the port of New York.

Unless—unless, Ziggy, too, had slipped up. Was that why he had suddenly clamped his mouth shut when he was discussing Waidler's efficiency?

Cherry felt sure that she was unraveling the mystery correctly. If so, the ambergris was somewhere in the purser's office right now.

But why hadn't Ziggy put such a valuable substance in the safe? Cherry could guess the answer to that one too. Because he hadn't known that several thousand dollars' worth of ambergris was among the old gentleman's effects.

Uncle Ben didn't believe in banks. But he was shrewd. He wouldn't label his share of the fine powder "ambergris" for the temptation of maids and stewards. How would he disguise his treasure when it wasn't on his person?

Cherry shook her head. That she couldn't know.

"Oh, dear," she moaned. "If only I could question Waidler; make him confess he didn't send all of old Mr. Paulding's possessions ashore with him last trip. Get him to tell me exactly what was overlooked in the last-minute rush."

Her hands were tied. Who was she to accuse Waidler of a minor transgression? Any minute now *he* was going to confront *her* with proof that she had violated two of the ship's regulations.

Someone tapped on her door. Cherry jumped up, bracing herself. "Here it comes!"

Then she marched stiff-shouldered to face her punishment.

~~~~~~

CHAPTER XIV

Waidler and Ziggy Are Evasive

WHEN CHERRY FLUNG OPEN THE DOOR OF HER CABIN she was not at all surprised to see Waidler standing there.

But she *was* surprised when he simply handed her a cable and started off again back to the main corridor.

Cherry could not stand the suspense another second. She called out, "Please, Waidler. I'd like to talk to you. Have you a minute?"

"No, I haven't," he flung back over one stooped shoulder, but he stopped in the narrow passageway. Cherry hurried after him.

"Waidler," she sputtered. "I just want to say . . . I just want to know . . . well, I mean, you did see me last night, didn't you?"

His eyes were blank under the heavy, beetling brows. "Last night? I guess I did if you were around. I don't remember. Haven't time to notice what the ship's nurse does or doesn't do."

Cherry's knees went wobbly with relief. Then he wasn't going to report her after all! "W-Waidler," she stammered, "I-I only did it for Timmy. He cried and cried for his panda. Then when I brought it back I felt it would be nicer if he thought his mother had gotten it for him." She went on in a rush of words as he listened stolidly:

"Timmy has a nurse, you see. His mother has never had the fun of taking care of him. He hadn't any confidence in her. But he has now that he thinks she dove into the deep part of the pool for his Fuzzy-Wuzzy."

"I don't know what *you*'re talking about," Waidler interrupted brusquely. *"Tim* told me his mother rescued his panda from the pool. As far as I'm concerned the passenger is always right."

Cherry impulsively grabbed his hand and shook it hard. "You're just about the nicest man I ever knew. And to think when I first came on board I thought you were horrid. Why were you so mean to me, Waidler?"

Waidler's dark brows were inverted V's of surprise. "Me mean? I've never said a cross word to anybody in my whole life. You must be crazy!"

Cherry laughed, almost hysterically. "I guess you didn't realize it then. But I was on the verge of tears that first day when you were so—well, abrupt with me."

Waidler thoughtfully stroked his chin with a stubby thumb. "Well, now, that's what the other nurse said to me. Said I hurt her feelings. Guess you nurses are awful sensitive. I've got two daughters just about your age. Why would I want to hurt a nice young lady's feelings?"

The steward shuffled his feet, embarrassed. "Guess I'll have to mind my manners after this. I'm always in such a hurry I don't know what I'm doing or saying half the time. Like at Willemstad last trip—" He stopped, and like Ziggy, clamped his mouth shut.

"I can imagine things were pretty hectic for you," Cherry put in quickly. "Getting a dying passenger ashore amid all the confusion of docking. I should think you might easily have overlooked something when you were packing Mr. Paulding's effects. A small package, for instance, away back in one of his drawers?"

Two red spots appeared on Waidler's prominent cheekbones. He scowled darkly, muttering, "Nothing of the kind. Emptied his drawers myself. And it seems to me if I can mind my own business, you can mind yours."

He darted away and Cherry thought: "Well, that's that. I've only succeeded in making him mad at me again. And I can't say I blame him. One good turn deserves another, but, instead, I insulted the nice old sea dog."

Sea dog! That started another train of thought. A seasoned sailor would know ambergris when he saw it—or smelled it. Had the temptation been too much for Waidler? Had he figured that finders were keepers, especially in the case of a dying man?

Jan's uncle, an old sea dog himself, might not have tipped the steward lavishly, and with good reason, too.

Until he sold his share of the ambergris he would have had to live on the few hundred dollars in his money belt.

Kirk Monroe had told Cherry the evening before that passengers' tips averaged about ten dollars a day. That was a lot of money unless you had a lot to throw around.

Cherry, remembering her embarrassed offering of a quarter that first day, felt sure that undertipping was the reason Waidler hadn't gotten on with old Mr. Paulding. Perhaps that had served as a sop to his conscience if he *had* pocketed the ambergris. To Waidler, not knowing that it was priceless *ambre blanc,* it might have represented only his just due. A less perfect type of ambergris, Jan had said, sold for only a few dollars an ounce.

Cherry, of course, didn't know exactly how many ounces had been Mr. Paulding's share. All she knew was that his partner had sold his portion for around five thousand dollars. But Waidler couldn't have known that.

Cherry shrugged. "I'm letting my imagination run away with me. Waidler is probably perfectly innocent. The thing to do is to try to find out from Kirk Monroe if the old gentleman said anything before he died that might be a clue to where he kept the ambergris. But first I think I'll have a talk with Ziggy."

Cherry had a perfectly good excuse to visit the purser's office. She had not yet had time to take a written inventory of the medical refrigerator. Ziggy was sitting at his desk when she came in.

"Hello," he said mournfully. "I suppose you've heard what happened last night?"

Cherry nodded. "Are we allowed to discuss the mystery, or is that scuttlebutt?"

"Scuttlebutt!" The wiry little steward pounded the desk with his calloused hands. "It's gone beyond scuttlebutt, Miss Cherry. The Old Man's on the rampage. Had me up there all morning."

"Thank goodness I escaped that," Cherry said inwardly. "If the captain's already on the rampage I wouldn't have had a prayer." Aloud, she said:

"Was anything taken this time?"

"Nothing. Absolutely nothing. At least," Ziggy finished evasively, "nothing of any importance. A carbon copy of such an unimportant letter that I didn't even mention it to the Old Man."

Cherry couldn't help wondering about that. Ziggy should have reported even the most minor loss to the captain. Why had he failed to do so? She asked him quietly:

"Can you remember what the letter was all about? It might be a clue, you know."

Ziggy snorted. "Nothing of the sort. I mean, I do remember the letter word for word. But there's not a clue in it, Miss Cherry. And don't you go asking me to repeat it to you. Because I won't. If you're smart you'll keep out of this. There are only four keys to this room. And you have one of them!"

Cherry's red cheeks burned under the implication that it was she who had taken the letter. For the second time that morning she was under suspicion. She said coolly, "If I had wanted to take anything I wouldn't have had to wait until last night. I could have done it any time I wanted to, Mr. Ziegler."

The normally good-natured purser relented then. "Don't pay any attention to me, Miss Cherry! I'm in such a state I'm beginning to suspect the Old Man himself. I hope whoever swiped that letter doesn't leave it lying around. If the captain ever saw it, I *would* be—" He stopped himself just in time. Shrewdly he finished with "I'd be hard put to explain why I didn't report it had been taken from the files."

"Why didn't you report it?" Cherry said mildly.

Ziggy spread his hands expressively. "You don't know the skipper. Hates details. That letter was a detail. If I'd mentioned it, he'd probably have had an attack of apoplexy. Very impatient man, the skipper. We old-timers learned long ago never to bother him with anything that wasn't important."

It sounded like a weak explanation to Cherry. And Ziggy's manner was evasive to say the least. While she checked the contents of the medical refrigerator, Cherry wondered why the letter had been stolen.

Ziggy sat at his desk, lost in thought. "It's the work of a practical joker," he said at last. "I probably mislaid that letter myself. Someone who has a master key, and what *he* thinks is a sense of humor, is behind all this. You run into crazy passengers like that every so often. Like the old man who died last trip. I always knew he was strange, but I didn't know he was crazy until I heard what he said just before he lost consciousness."

Cherry pricked up her ears. "What did he say, Ziggy? I'm interested in hearing about him; he was the uncle of the young Paulding girl in Suite 125–127, you know. She adored him, and I'm sure it would mean a great deal to her to know just what his last words were."

That, she reflected, smiling inwardly, was putting it mildly, but she didn't want to arouse the purser's suspicions.

Ziggy shook his head grimly. "If she wants to know, she'll have to ask the ship's surgeon. I'm just the pharmacist's mate when it comes to dying passengers." He got up and left the room.

Cherry decided that Ziggy was right. Jan herself would have to question Dr. Monroe. Even though it was now "Kirk" and "Cherry," he would never violate professional ethics and repeat what his patient had said.

After she had finished her inventory, Cherry went to the dispensary to check the supplies and the sterilization equipment. Then it was noon and time for her visit to Timmy.

Mrs. Crane looked exhausted by her four-hour stretch of duty. But she didn't utter a complaint. With Cherry looking on, she went through the routine of Timmy's care without mishap. Cherry complimented her enthusiastically.

"You're as good as any nurse's aide now. In another day or so I'll be pinning a handkerchief on your hair to show you've won your cap."

Mrs. Crane flushed with pleasure. "The doctor said Timmy couldn't go out on deck today because of the rise in his temperature last night. But he did say if it was normal all day Timmy could go up to the library and see the Christmas tree when it's lighted up this evening. That nice Mr. Landgraf offered to carry Timmy. That was really awfully sweet of him, don't you think?"

"Oh, did Timmy have a visitor this morning?" Cherry asked quickly.

"Oh, yes, Mr. Landgraf and Jan Paulding and her mother. He and Jan both offered to read to Timmy while I took a dip in the pool, but I refused. I was afraid Miss Cherry Ames would scold me if I left the room for even one minute."

Cherry laughed. "Well, you've earned a rest. I'll ask the steward to bring my lunch on the same tray with Timmy's. So you run along and have your swim. Unless I'm called elsewhere I'll be glad to stay with Timmy for a couple of hours."

Mrs. Crane thanked Cherry gratefully. "Then I'll just stay right on until two and have my lunch at the pool. You're a lamb, Cherry."

Timmy was so full of Christmas Eve excitement he could hardly eat. When Cherry told him it was her birthday too, he promptly offered to give her the entire contents of his toy box.

And then Cherry suddenly remembered the cable she had tucked into her uniform pocket hours ago. It was from her mother:

HAPPY BIRTHDAY DARLING. HAVE LOTS OF FUN.

A wave of homesickness swept over Cherry. If she were home now she and Charlie would be trimming the tree. There would be all sorts of mysterious whisperings as gifts were wrapped in the presence of everyone except the one who would open them on Christmas Day. Lost in thought she didn't hear what Timmy was saying until he repeated:

"I've got a piece of yellow paper too, Cherry. Listen to me! I've got a 'portant piece of yellow paper too."

"Have you?" Cherry smiled. "That's nice. Did somebody send you a cable wishing you a merry Christmas?"

Timmy shook his head. "No, it b'longs to Henry. He was reading it in that chair just like you're reading yours. Then Jan came in and he stuffed it in his pocket. But when he wasn't looking I took it out and hid it under my pillow."

"Timmy Crane," Cherry scolded. "You're a naughty boy. Give me that paper right away. I'll have Waidy return it to Henry when he comes for our trays."

"Okey-dokey," Timmy said cheerfully. "I just borrowed it cause it looked so nice and 'portant. But you've got to read it to me first. I could only read *some* of the words, like *milk.*"

Cherry laughed. "I don't think you read that one right. I can't imagine anyone used the word milk in a cable to Henry."

"Did so read it right," Tim shouted. "M-I-L-K spells milk!" He reached under his pillow and produced a crumpled piece of yellow paper.

It was not, Cherry saw at once, a cablegram. Then she almost shouted herself, when Timmy triumphantly pointed to four capital letters in the middle of the sheet. They did, indeed, spell milk, and the crumpled piece of yellow paper was the carbon copy of a letter signed:

"R. D. Ziegler, Ship's Purser."

CHAPTER XV

~~~~~~

Milk of Magnesia

CHERRY'S EYES ALMOST POPPED OUT OF HER HEAD. THIS, then, must be the missing letter.

"Read it," Tim yelled. "Read to me."

Cherry hesitated. Should she return the letter to the purser without finding out what it said? If she did, she might be letting a valuable clue slip through her fingers. She glanced swiftly at the name and address above the salutation. There could be no harm in reading that much of it.

One glance was enough for Cherry. The letter was addressed to:

> MR. JUAN CAMELOT, *Attorney-at-Law*
> Willemstad
> Curaçao

Jan's Uncle Benedict's lawyer!

164

"Read it," Timmy yelled for the third time. And Cherry did, swiftly, so that the words were jumbled together and made no sense at all to the little boy.

"What's so 'portant 'bout that?" he demanded in disgust. He returned to the more exciting topic of what Santa Claus was going to bring him.

As he rambled on with the long list of what he expected to find in his stocking the next morning, Cherry read the letter more carefully.

Dear Sir:

Due to an oversight on the part of a steward, certain items in the late Mr. Benedict Paulding's medicine cabinet were not included in the effects sent ashore at the time of his disembarkation on Tuesday, December 12th. These items are enclosed herewith. They are:

> 1 *Gold-plated Safety Razor*
> 1 *Used Razor Blade*
> 1 *New " "*
> 1 *Toothbrush*
> 1 *Can Tooth Powder*
> 1 *Bottle Milk of Magnesia (16 ounces)*
> 1 *Comb (2 Teeth Missing)*
> 1 *Pair Military Hairbrushes*

I myself am guilty of neglecting to turn these items into the Home Office at the Port of New York. I am therefore sending them to you by messenger when we next dock in Willemstad, Tuesday, December 26th. I trust this is satisfactory.

Cherry stared at the fifth item: *1 Can Tooth Powder*. Perhaps *it* contained the missing ambergris! If so, it was perfectly safe in the purser's locked desk where he kept all trivia connected with the passengers. She had caught a glimpse of that drawer earlier when he put away a handkerchief and compact a waitress had discovered left behind on one of the dining-room tables. The deep drawer was filled with large and small sealed, brown-paper packages, all carefully labeled and dated.

In one of them was Jan's ambergris! So the mystery was over. All Jan had to do was request the purser to hand over her uncle's toilet articles to her, his heir.

But would it be as simple as that? Ziggy might refuse, even when confronted with the carbon copy of the letter to Mr. Camelot. And rightly so. There was some legal technicality that prevented heirs from inheriting anything until after the will had been probated. Jan had said that her uncle's will would not be probated until her arrival in Willemstad.

So what was their next step? Whoever had twice broken into the purser's office would surely make another search. This time, he might be successful.

If that mysterious person was, as Cherry was beginning to suspect, Mr. Henry Landgraf, he now knew what she knew: that some of old Mr. Paulding's possessions were still aboard ship. Like Cherry, he would immediately think of the tooth-powder can . . . a perfect, innocent-looking container for priceless ambergris.

Cherry could hardly wait to consult with Jan. At last it was two o'clock and Mrs. Crane came back right on the hour, excited and flushed.

"Run along, Cherry," she said. "And don't come back at four. I'm going to be really brave and try to cope all by myself." She giggled. "I'm glad you can't get too far away from me, though."

Cherry decided that she had better obtain the ship's surgeon's approval before turning complete care of Timmy over to his pretty young mother.

She found Kirk in his office two doors beyond.

"Hello," he greeted her. "Where have you been keeping yourself? If I hadn't seen your entries in the sick-bay log I wouldn't have known there was a nurse aboard."

Cherry pretended to sulk. "After all, Dr. Monroe, it *is* Sunday. And, I might add, the day before Christmas. Not to mention the fact—or *also,* as Timmy would say, my birthday!"

"Cherry!" He pumped her hand up and down. "And the gift shop would be closed until this evening, so I can't buy you a present!"

"I don't want a present." Cherry smiled. "What I want you to do is let me turn Timmy over to his mother from now on. It's not that I want to get out of a task, it's just that it's good for her—for both of them." Then she explained about Timmy's grandmother and Nanny.

Kirk nodded approvingly. "You're a good little psychologist, Cherry. And there's no reason why his mother shouldn't assume full responsibility now. Even a teenager like Jan could nurse him without too much risk. If his temperature doesn't go up tonight, we'll take him off sulfa as a Christmas present. And let him go on deck. It's a shame he's missing all this lovely tropical weather. As a matter of fact, let's prescribe a sun bath for him this afternoon. It can't possibly do him any harm and I think probably will do him a lot of good."

"That's what I think," Cherry said. "He's hardly coughing at all now and he's not nearly so hoarse."

Kirk Monroe chuckled. "If he didn't insist upon talking so much he would probably have gotten over his laryngitis much sooner. He's a regular magpie, that one!"

He's like a magpie in more ways than one, Cherry thought, remembering the letter Tim had filched from Henry Landgraf's pocket. She flushed guiltily. That letter was still in her own pocket. Ethically speaking, she should return it to the purser at once. But she didn't like to do that until she had shown it to Jan.

Suddenly it struck Cherry that the letter shouldn't be given to either Ziggy or Jan. She should take it straight to the captain herself. For it was irrevocable proof that Mr. Henry Landgraf had taken it from the purser's office the night before.

But there was good old Rule 6:

"The ship's nurse must always be diplomatic, cooperative and courteous in her relationship with a passenger, an officer, or a member of the crew."

And, the next one: "When an equivocal question arises, the nurse must not assume any responsibility whatsoever. She must immediately refer the passenger, the officer, or the member of the crew to the ship's surgeon."

Before she knew it Cherry had handed over Ziggy's letter and was blurting out the whole story.

"Ambergris!" Kirk interrupted once.

"Yes, ambergris," Cherry said. "Fantastic, but true."

"It's a fantastic substance all right," Kirk agreed. "Especially the much-sought-after fossil ambergris. They say that effete Oriental potentates value highly the flavor of a drop of the tincture in their hot coffee. And there's a legend in the Indies and Moslem countries that it has the same life-giving qualities that Ponce de Leon's Florida Water was supposed to have. In olden times the maharajahs treasured it in sealed caskets as they did their gold and precious stones. Their descendants can now sell this form of superrefined ambergris for fabulous sums."

"Then Jan's *ambre blanc,*" Cherry put in, "may be very valuable?"

"I imagine so," Kirk agreed. "You see a little of the pulverized stuff goes a long way. When I was a kid a chemist friend of mine let me watch him prepare the tincture. First he crushed a small stone of it with mortar and pestle. Pretty much the way you prepare Tim's sulfa." He smiled. "Then he added alcohol at 96° in a proportion of 8 liters to 1,000 grams of powdered ambergris. The mixture was allowed to stand, with occasional stirring, in an open container for eight days. Then the alcohol was poured off and another

8 ounces poured over the residue. After eight washings, my chemist friend had 40 liters of the tincture which he filtered into another container and left to age in a warm place for about six months. Then he started all over again with the settling."

"You mean what was left of the original 1,000 grams?" Cherry demanded incredulously.

"That's right," Kirk grinned. "It goes on almost endlessly like the story of the ants who kept going into the granary and bringing out another grain of wheat. After the chemists exhaust the settling—and I do mean exhaust—it is dried and ground and then used in sachet powders. They literally don't waste a grain of it."

Cherry sighed. "Well, I'm glad you know all about it. I couldn't quite believe it was as valuable as Jan claims it is. What does it smell like, Kirk?"

"That depends on the quality," he told her. "A highly refined lot of *ambre blanc* would be faintly reminiscent of incense in a church, plus the seaweedy mustiness of the tide on the high seas. That's a much more exotic odor than the tide on a beach, you know. There's a muskiness through it all and sometimes a trace of an aroma that makes you think of expensively blended tobacco."

Cherry went on with her story then. Kirk listened soberly and when she had finished he said, "There's nothing we can do, Cherry, except advise Jan to cable the lawyer at once to come aboard in person and get that sealed envelope. A messenger might be intercepted."

"But," Cherry protested, "why can't we lay the matter before the captain? Make him put the package in his own safe? Surely, he would when we tell him it contains priceless ambergris!"

Kirk threw back his head, roaring with laughter. "You *are* a landlubber, Cherry Ames! In the first place, the Old Man would have apoplexy if he heard you were probing into the passengers' personal affairs. In the second, leaving you out of it, he would immediately ask for my resignation. Shipboard protocol forbids my activity in any department except the medical department. Reporting our suspicions to him would be like telling him how to avoid a collision at sea. We leave radar to him, and he leaves sick bay to us. We're subjects of a little autocracy, if you like, but that's the way it is."

Cherry sighed. "I'm so afraid Mr. Henry Landgraf will steal that ambergris before we dock on Tuesday. If he does, Jan will have to give up her hopes of becoming an artist."

Kirk grinned. "You don't *know* that Mr. Landgraf is the villain in the case. Someone else might have crumpled up that letter and thrown it away, thinking there was no clue in it as to the whereabouts of the ambergris. Mr. Landgraf might have picked it up and read it out of idle curiosity. Seems like a nice enough fellow to me. Spends a lot of time amusing Tim—even offered to carry him up to see the tree this evening."

"But don't you see?" Cherry wailed. "He's just using Timmy so he can have opportunities to search that cabin."

"I wouldn't be too sure of that," Kirk Monroe said mildly. "Tim has impressed everyone who entered his presence into service. He even got me playing 'hot and cold' in the search for his Fuzzy-Wuzzy. And to think it was at the bottom of the pool all along."

Cherry sucked in her breath. How much did Dr. Monroe know about that?

But the surgeon went on easily, "I gather his mother finally retrieved the panda last night. Can't imagine why one of the pool attendants didn't discover it before."

"It was lying on the bottom in the shadow of the diving board," Cherry blurted. Too late, she could have bitten off her tongue.

Fortunately the young doctor did not notice her blunder. "So that was the answer," he said incuriously, adding, "I imagine you want to go along now and have a chat with Jan Paulding about that cable. Unofficially, in an advisory capacity only, I'll help every way I can." He stared thoughtfully down at his hands. "I rather hope, Cherry, that Mr. Camelot won't find any ambergris in that sealed package. If he does, he will almost certainly report both Ziggy's and Waidler's negligence to the captain."

He shook his head. "They both have excellent records as loyal and conscientious employees of long standing. It would be a shame if their careers had to end in disgrace due to such minor infractions of duty." He pointed to the itemized list in the letter. "Less honest persons would have dumped that stuff overboard without a qualm."

Cherry hadn't thought about that angle of Jan's problem. Now she saw all too clearly that this bit of scuttlebutt must never reach the captain's ears. She took the bull by the horns:

"Kirk," she said hesitantly, "you can be a big help right now by answering one simple question. If you don't want to answer me, I'll get Jan to ask you the same question. Did her uncle say anything before he lost consciousness? Anything at all significant?"

Kirk Monroe ran his long, surgeon's fingers along the edge of his glass-topped desk. "Now that you remind me, he did say something which may or may not be significant. At the time I thought his mind was wandering, because shortly after that he lapsed into a coma. At first he merely complained of a pain in his chest, then when his breathing became more labored, he beckoned to me with one hand and pointed to the bathroom with the other. I could hardly make out what he was saying, but it sounded like:

" 'Milk of magnesia. Please, Doc, give me milk of magnesia.' "

"I remember," Kirk went on, "Ziggy grunted and tapped his forehead. I felt the same way about the request. What good would milk of magnesia do to a man dying with a blood clot in his lung?"

"Not much," Cherry admitted. "Is that *all* he said?"

"That's all he had time for," Kirk told her. "It all happened very quickly, I had hardly time to send for the nurse and Ziggy. Then his lawyer came aboard and took him ashore. I signed the necessary papers, and that was that."

Cherry suddenly jumped up. "Oh, Kirk," she cried. "Don't you see? Milk of magnesia bottles are generally made of cloudy, blue glass. You couldn't tell, unless you examined them carefully, whether they contained a powder or a liquid. The magnesia itself often forms a white powdery crust around the neck of the bottle. What a perfect hiding place for a pint of priceless ambergris!"

CHAPTER XVI

Jan Sets a Trap

DR. KIRK MONROE STARED AT CHERRY. "THAT'S THE answer, of course. Old Mr. Paulding put his ambergris powder into an empty magnesia bottle." He frowned suddenly. "Wait a minute. Let's not jump to conclusions, Cherry. Mr. Paulding *did* suffer from chronic dyspepsia, especially after meals. He ate like a horse," Kirk remembered with a grin. "All the wrong things for a man of his age. Had an attack the first night out— that's how I got to know him before he was stricken with pulmonary thrombosis. Most of the other passengers—even the ship's nurse—were seasick, but the old gentleman had nothing but a good old-fashioned bellyache. Ziggy had given him rhubarb and soda before I arrived. However, he insisted that milk of magnesia was the only medication that ever did him any good."

"Oh," Cherry sighed disappointedly. "Then you think Mr. Paulding really wanted milk of magnesia when he asked you for it the day he died? That he thought he was simply having another attack of dyspepsia?"

"I'm afraid so," Dr. Monroe said slowly. "I gave him a bottle and a package of tablets that first night and he chewed the tablets like candy after that. Was always running out of them and asking for more. It got on Waidler's nerves, the way the old gentleman was forever chewing those tablets. It was Waidler's opinion that Mr. Paulding should be put on a gruel-and-milk-toast diet." Kirk laughed. "Even the maid who cleaned his cabin complained to me that she got sick of hearing about his weak stomach. It was pretty ridiculous, the whole thing. If the old man had as much discomfort as he claimed he did, I feel sure he would have eaten more moderately. But he never hesitated to top off creamed oysters and lobster Newburg with a couple of fried soft-shell crabs."

"Oh, my goodness." Cherry laughed. "He must have had a cast-iron stomach."

Kirk stood up. "He was a queer duck all right, but Ziggy and I liked him. He was fond of spinning yarns about his adventures on the high seas. Timmy would have worshiped the ground—or I should say, deck—he walked on. I hated to lose that patient, but I imagine he had had a fuller and more satisfactory life than most of us."

He followed Cherry out into the corridor. "Promised to look in on Mrs. Paulding. Wants me to listen to her heart, although I can't tell you why."

When Dr. Monroe had assured Jan's mother that he could hear no murmurs, Jan pulled Cherry into the other room and closed the door carefully behind them.

"Have you found out anything?" she whispered excitedly.

Cherry, remembering the strict rules about gossip, said cautiously, "I came across some information which proves you were right. Some of your uncle's possessions were not sent ashore with him. The purser has them in a sealed package in his locked desk."

Jan started for the door. "How wonderful! I'll get him to give me that package right now."

Cherry stopped her. "He won't do it, honey. Legally he must turn it over to your uncle's lawyer until the will has been probated."

Jan tensed with disappointment. "Oh, Cherry, I can't stand it. That means waiting until Tuesday. And suppose the ambergris isn't in that sealed package? I'll leave the ship at Willemstad and then I'll never have another chance to look for it."

"There's only one thing you can do," Cherry told her. "Cable Mr. Camelot to come aboard as soon as the *Julita* docks. He can open the package then and there. If there is no sign of the ambergris, your lawyer can put the matter before the captain and have the ship systematically searched."

"Why didn't I think of that before?" Jan broke in suddenly. "I can go to the captain right now. Now that I *know* some of Uncle Ben's things were left behind I can make him open that package. The captain of a ship has supreme authority while at sea. *He* doesn't have to wait until the will is probated. Besides," she finished shrewdly, "he's responsible for the delay and worry about that ambergris. The steamship line was at fault for not sending everything ashore with my uncle."

Cherry felt sick all over. If Jan went to the captain both Ziggy and Waidler would be up for sharp reprimands, if not dismissal. Kirk, as the attending physician during the patient's disembarkation, might well be dragged into it. The jobs of three people might be threatened merely to satisfy the whim of an impatient sixteen-year-old girl. After all, Tuesday was only two days off.

Cherry knew now she would have to break another rule and tell Jan the whole story. She would have to appeal to the girl's sense of fairness.

Cherry took a deep breath, wishing that she were more of an accomplished orator. Gently, she pulled Jan down on the sofa beside her.

"Jan," she began soberly, "you have every right to go to the captain. But I hope that when I have finished my story you will decide against it."

Jan's hazel eyes were wide with bewilderment. "What story? I don't understand. Why shouldn't I go to the captain?"

Cherry began at the beginning and somehow made Jan listen until she had finished. When Jan heard that the purser's office had twice been broken into she was all for racing up to the captain without wasting another minute:

"It's Timmy's Henry, of course. He may have already stolen that sealed package. If not, he'll certainly get it tonight, Cherry. I've simply *got* to go to the captain."

Firmly, Cherry pulled her down beside her. She had not much hope of enlisting Jan's sympathy for either Ziggy or Waidler. Jan did not know the former, and had said she disliked the latter.

"There's no way I can convince you of what undue hardship disgrace would cause those two men," Cherry said. "They might never be able to get another job at sea. It would break their hearts. Do you think they deserve such a punishment for merely overlooking a few toilet articles? The whole kit and kaboodle couldn't amount to more than a dollar or two."

Jan bit her thumb between sharp white teeth. "That old bear of a Waidy! He grows on you. I disliked him intensely at first, but now I wish Mother would hire him as our butler. He tells the most marvelous sea stories you ever heard, Cherry, and do you know? He's got ten children ranging from eight months to daughters around your age! He adores children and says he'd like to have ten more!"

Cherry felt a surge of relief. Here at least was an opening wedge. She was quick to press her point. "It's going to be awfully hard on his family if he loses his job."

"Oh, Mother'll hire him," Jan said carelessly. "She doesn't like our present butler anyway. He's not very sympathetic with her headaches. And Waidy is. He hovered around her breakfast tray this morning like a mother hen. You'd think he wouldn't worry about the appetite of anyone as plump as my mother!"

"Do you honestly think Waidy would enjoy a shore job?" Cherry put in quietly. "He's as salty as the sea itself. And do you think it's right that he should be dishonorably discharged after all the years of faithful service he's given this line?"

Jan, looking like a tawny young lioness, began to pace the rug.

"It's his future against mine," she muttered. "If only we could be sure that the ambergris would be safe until we docked at Willemstad!" She came to a sudden halt in front of Cherry. "Tell me again what those toilet articles are."

Cherry repeated the list, ending with, "Until Dr. Monroe told me that your uncle suffered from dyspepsia, I hoped he'd kept it in the milk-of-magnesia bottle."

"Dyspepsia?" Jan's blond eyebrows shot up in surprise. "But that's perfectly silly, Cherry. Uncle Ben had a cast-iron stomach. During our walks through Central Park he would tuck away enormous quantities of popcorn, ice cream, peanuts, and sarsaparilla, especially sarsaparilla. He considered it the finest of all tonics. At one time he owned a plantation in Jamaica where they grew the stuff; tropical smilax, I think he called it. They exported the dried roots, and Uncle Ben said he made a lot of money."

Cherry pricked up her ears. "Then he didn't have the habit of chewing milk of magnesia tablets?"

Jan relaxed into laughter. "You didn't know Uncle Ben! I doubt if anyone could have made him take medicine in any form. His theory was that Nature knew best. If you craved something, no matter how fantastic, that was the very thing your system needed. I'll bet if he ever had an upset stomach he would have chewed grass the way a dog does."

Cherry joined in Jan's laughter. "Well, he couldn't get any grass at sea, and I don't suppose the *Julita* is stocked with either seaweed or sarsaparilla. So he had to chew milk of magnesia tablets." Suddenly Cherry sobered. "Oh, I see it all now! What a dumb bunny I was not to have seen it before. I was right the first time, Jan. The ambergris *is* in that blue-glass pint bottle."

Jan stared at her. "What makes you so sure? It was completely out of character for my uncle to have had a bottle of milk of magnesia in his possession. *I* think your purser made a mistake; mixed up the contents of another passenger's medicine cabinet with Uncle Ben's."

Cherry grinned. "It was out of character for him to own milk of magnesia, but it was completely *in* character for him to have gone to fantastic lengths to make sure that nobody guessed that the blue bottle contained a powder, not a liquid. Don't you see, Jan? He put on an act from start to finish. He was shrewd enough to know that anyone who saw him eat quantities of indigestible food would know he had a cast-iron stomach and wonder why he kept a bottle of milk of magnesia on hand. *Unless* he complained constantly of dyspepsia! As Dr. Monroe said only a short while ago:

" 'If the old man had as much discomfort as he claimed he did, I feel sure he would have eaten more moderately.'

"My guess is," Cherry went on, "that your uncle was afraid an old sea dog like Waidler might discover his precious ambergris while working around the stateroom. Only a seasoned sailor would recognize the substance and its delicate odor. So, the very first night, your Uncle Ben pretended to have an attack of dyspepsia. He demanded a bottle of milk of magnesia."

"Then," Jan took up the story excitedly, "he poured the magnesia down the sink and filled the bottle with ambergris. Oh, it all dovetails perfectly. The very first day at sea I asked our maid if she had taken care of the gentleman in 141 who had died at Curaçao last trip. She didn't know I was his niece, of course, and she said:

" 'I certainly did. And a most peculiar old gentleman, he was, too. Wouldn't let me wipe up his bathroom, I'll have you know, miss. Said I was a clumsy girl and would be sure to drop things and break them on the tiled floor.' "

Cherry jumped up. "So now we *know*. Oh, Jan! All your troubles are over. By this time, Tuesday, your lawyer will be cabling big South American perfume manufacturers for bids. He may sell your ambergris for thousands and thousands of dollars."

"I'm not hoping for a fortune," Jan said. "Uncle said that it wouldn't take much to make the property at Piscadera Bay salable. He didn't plan to do anything to the house. It would have to be completely modernized anyway. The beach is the valuable part of the property."

Cherry smiled. "Someday we may meet again when you're a famous artist."

But Jan didn't smile back. "My dream is just as far away as ever, Cherry," she said tautly. "There's no sense in counting chickens before they're hatched. How do we know Timmy's pirate friend won't get that ambergris before we dock at Willemstad? I'll send a cable to Mr. Camelot, of course, but Tuesday may be too late. By that time the sealed package may contain everything except the only thing we want, a one-pint bottle of milk of magnesia!"

Cherry groaned inwardly. She could tell by the tense expression on Jan's face that she still felt she should report the whole matter to the captain.

Desperately Cherry said, "He, or whoever it was who broke into the purser's office twice, doesn't know what *we* know. It seems to me, if he took anything he'd take the tooth powder can. That would be the most logical thing to take."

Jan shook her head. "I feel pretty sure now that Mr. Henry Morgan Landgraf is none other than my uncle's ex-partner. He knew Uncle Ben had the *ambre blanc* when he sailed on the *Julita* two weeks ago. It wouldn't fit into a tooth powder can. Uncle believed in traveling light. He probably bought a sample-sized can of tooth powder in a ten cent store." She laughed mirthlessly. "No, Cherry, I know you think I'm selfish, and I guess I am." She raised her voice defiantly. "But I'm going to see the captain the first thing in the morning. I don't care if it is Christmas!"

Cherry said hotly: "You *are* selfish, Jan Paulding."

Jan stalked to the French windows and stood there looking out unseeingly at the glorious tropical sunset.

Cherry started for the door. There was nothing more she could say or do. Oh, why had she taken Jan into her confidence; why had she broken the ship's scuttlebutt rule? She had known all along that this determined young girl had a merciless, selfish, one-track mind. Or, she *should* have known it.

Jan had deliberately goaded her mother into a migraine attack. She had used sick little Timmy as an excuse to search his room. She had virtually, if not actually, lied to Cherry more than once.

Just reviewing the evidence made Cherry lose control of her temper. "I've been a complete fool," she said in a loud, clear voice, not caring who heard. "I should never have offered to help you. And certainly I should never have trusted you. Go ahead and report the purser and Waidler to the captain. No doubt, I'll be dismissed too. That should make your happiness complete, Jan Paulding."

For answer, Jan turned suddenly, her finger to her lips. Then she yawned elaborately and strolled away from the window. Once in the far corner of the room she hissed:

"That man was listening out there on deck. Mr. Landgraf. He just went back down to where Timmy's having a sun bath. I don't know how much he heard, but anyway, he's sure now that I'm going to the captain. Of course, I'm not going to do anything of the kind, Cherry. I'm no tattletale. I'm selfish, yes, but not that selfish. I saw something move on the other side of that French door. So I deliberately said I was going to the captain tomorrow. Don't you see, Cherry? That means he must act tonight if he wants to get the ambergris before I do. So we'll simply set a trap and catch him in the act."

Cherry gulped. "Tr-trap? What kind of trap?"

Jan shrugged airily. "It's the only way, Cherry. You told me yourself you have a key to the purser's office. So tonight during the Christmas Eve excitement, you'll lock me safely inside. When Tim's pirate friend comes sneaking in, I'll wait until he's jimmied the lock on the desk drawer. Then just as he's about to depart with my ambergris, I'll simply take it away from him. That way, none of your friends will be involved. I won't even report Henry Landgraf to the captain. After all, he's not a common, ordinary thief or he would have swiped the passengers' jewels and money when he rifled the safe."

Cherry burst into rather hysterical laughter. "And how on earth, Jan Paulding," she gasped, "do you think you're going to take anything away from that big, powerful man?"

Jan looked blank.

"The whole scheme is preposterous," Cherry said emphatically. "If anyone hides in the purser's office tonight, it'll be Cherry Ames."

"All right," Jan promptly agreed. "You do it. But how on earth, Nurse Ames," she mimicked, "do you think you're going to take a bottle of milk of magnesia away from that big, powerful man?"

Cherry grinned. "I couldn't, of course, any more than you could." She sobered. "But there must be some way out of it, Jan. Let's both think about it quietly and meet again after dinner. Between us, we should be able to cook up a plan."

Jan moved her pale eyebrows expressively. "What about between now and then?"

"We don't have to worry about anything until nine this evening," Cherry answered. "Ziggy is in and out of his office almost constantly until his bedtime. The only hitch would be if we were both called to emergency duty in sick bay. In that case, I'd tell you."

"And," Jan told her, "I'd think up some excuse so I could be lurking outside the purser's office until the coast was clear."

"That's right," Cherry said. "Furthermore, I'll have an opportunity to keep my eye on Mr. Landgraf for quite a while after dinner tonight. He's going to carry Timmy up to the library to see the Christmas tree and hang up his stocking."

"Wonderful," Jan cried enthusiastically. "You know," she added, "I can't help liking that man, Cherry. Somehow, I honestly do think if he knew the ambergris belonged to me, he'd give it to me."

"Well, if he is, as you suspect, your uncle's ex-partner," Cherry said doubtfully, "he must know that you're his heir."

"Not necessarily," Jan returned. "For one thing, Uncle Ben was very closemouthed about his private affairs. For another, he'd had absolutely nothing to do with any of us for years and years. I was a tiny baby the last time he saw my father, and he never wrote a line to any of the family. He told me himself he didn't know why he called on Mother last month. It just seemed like a good idea at the time, I guess. He didn't like either of my parents and he wasn't the least bit sentimental. So as far as his partner was concerned, Uncle Ben just didn't have any family to leave his share of the ambergris to."

"But Mr. Landgraf knows about you now, doesn't he?" Cherry countered.

"Of course not," Jan said. "He doesn't even know my last name. Timmy introduced us, and you know how *he* feels about last names." Jan giggled. "Tim simply said: 'Henry, Jan's that dumb girl I was telling you about. She couldn't find anything if it was on the end of her nose.'"

Jan sobered suddenly. "But he *does* know I've been searching Timmy's cabin. He caught me the very first day." She shivered reminiscently. "He stared at me with those cold blue, blue eyes of his and said mockingly: 'Looking for something?' He scared me so I jumped up and ran out of the room as though he were a ghost."

"Well," Cherry said, "if he scared you like that in broad daylight, just think how you'd feel tonight in the pitch dark of the purser's office!"

Jan went on as though she hadn't heard. "He frightens me and fascinates me at the same time. I guess it's his looks. I'm supposed to be a descendant of Theodosia Burr—you know, the one whose ship mysteriously disappeared off the Carolinian coast in the early nineteenth century. Granddaddy told me that *his* grandmother strongly suspected that Theodosia ran away with a pirate." Jan giggled. "Oh, you know what I mean, Cherry. Henry Landgraf has the same rough charm Uncle Benedict had. And from where he sits, now that Uncle's dead, that ambergris is in public domain."

"Perhaps. And like the old-time pirates, it's every man for himself on the high seas," Cherry said thoughtfully.

"That's what I think," Jan agreed. "Ashore he probably wouldn't even commit a minor traffic violation. But we're not ashore. We're steaming toward the Spanish Main on the bright blue Caribbean Sea!"

~~~~~~

CHAPTER XVII

A Tree for Timmy

CHERRY HERSELF SHIVERED AS SHE SLIPPED OUT INTO the corridor. The way imaginative Jan put it, you could almost hear the wild chant of a pirate crew below decks, and the flapping of a skull and crossbones at the top of the mast.

And Tim's Henry did look like a pirate; one of the *nice* ones in Dr. Monroe's book, it was true. But all pirates were ruthless, weren't they?

There was no doubt in Cherry's mind that tonight of all nights—Christmas Eve—the purser's office would be broken into for the third time. Would Jan's dream of becoming an artist end with the tropical dawn of tomorrow, Christmas?

"I've got to do something," Cherry thought as she showered and changed into a fresh uniform. "Oh, if only everyone weren't so involved in that ambergris!"

Jan and Ziggy and Waidler—perhaps even herself and Kirk—not to mention the mysterious Henry Landgraf. How could the problem be solved without hurting someone?

"Jan's a good sport," Cherry decided as she hurried down the corridor for a peek at Timmy before dinner. "It was awfully hard for her to decide not to report the whole business to the captain. She deserves that ambergris!"

Timmy had momentarily discarded his stocking list in favor of another exciting topic.

"You know what, Cherry?" he greeted her. "We're going to have a fire drill tomorrow morning. Christmas and everything."

"How do you know?" Cherry asked doubtfully.

"Waidy tole me. In school we have a bell that rings and rings and rings. Then there's a gong and we all march out. But on board ship it's dif-frunt. You'll see. They'll put a little piece of paper under your plate at dinner tonight. I got one on my tray. See?" He handed the little card of printed instructions to Cherry.

Cherry glanced at it and nodded.

Timmy pointed importantly to the larger card on his cabin wall. "That tells you what seat you sit in on what lifeboat," he announced, just as though Cherry couldn't read. "*Also*, it tells you if the lifeboat is forward or aft or amidships." Tim giggled. "Waidy says it's lots of fun cause the passengers get all mixed up and go in the wrong places when the gong rings. But *I* won't. I know just 'zactly where my boat is. *Also*, when they swing my boat down I'm going to get into it. You're not 'posed to 'less there's a real fire, but I'm going to. Cause Waidy says there are boxes of crackers and chocolate bars in every boat."

"Did Waidy show you how to put on your life preserver?" Cherry asked.

"No," Timmy said. "But he showed Mummy how and she showed me."

"We had a lot of fun learning," Mrs. Crane added, "didn't we, Tim?"

Timmy nodded. "You'd better show Cherry how, Mummy. She can't swim as good as you can. She might get 'most drownded like my Fuzzy. Fuzzy," he told Cherry, "is hanging up his stocking too. Henry bought us both red ones with bells on 'em in the shop upstairs. When are we going to see the tree?"

"After dinner," Cherry said. "When I've finished eating I'll come back and stay with you until your mother's through. Then we'll all go up to the library together."

"Henry too," Tim said. "He's going to carry me piggyback. I'm going to pe-tend he's my llama. Do you know what a llama is, Cherry? He's a camel, only in Peru they don't have humps so they call 'em llamas. But they're *very* fuzzy."

"My goodness," Cherry said to Mrs. Crane. "Timmy has picked up so much information this trip he could afford to skip school for a year."

"It's that nice Mr. Landgraf," Mrs. Crane said. "He's the most fascinating man, Cherry. Like Timmy, I could sit here all day and listen to him talk." She added in a whisper: "He's going to teach me how to dive, so Tim won't suspect that it was you who dived for his panda."

Cherry took a deep breath and let it out slowly. She got up and walked into the adjoining room, beckoning to Mrs. Crane to follow. Then she whispered, "Does Mr. Landgraf know I was in the pool last night?"

"Oh, yes," Mrs. Crane admitted. "He *saw* you. But he didn't give our secret away. Tim still thinks *I* got his Fuzzy."

Weak-kneed, Cherry sank down on the sofa. Mrs. Crane, of course, didn't know that the swimming pool was out of bounds for the ship's nurse. But seafaring Mr. Henry Landgraf undoubtedly did. Anytime he wanted to put Cherry out of the running all he had to do was report her disobedience to the captain.

How much had he heard of her conversation with Jan while Tim was sunbathing? Did he know now that Timmy had given the carbon copy of that letter to Cherry? Was he as certain as she and Jan were that the ambergris was in the milk-of-magnesia bottle? Picking the lock on the purser's desk drawer would be child's play to a man who had expertly twirled the dials on the safe their first day at sea. Those strong, deft fingers could probably unseal that brown paper package and remove the cloudy blue bottle without leaving any trace that the contents of the late Mr. Paulding's medicine cabinet had been rifled.

If he'd had more time on Friday he undoubtedly would have replaced the valuables in the safe so that no one would ever have known it had been broken into.

Cherry quickly made up her mind. Jan was right. Somehow they must set a trap and catch him in the act tonight. As long as nothing had been stolen, the captain would not think it necessary to put an officer on night duty in the purser's office. He would naturally think, as Ziggy did, that the breaking and entering had been done by a passenger with a skeleton key—and a warped sense of humor. Now that this passenger had had his fun with the purser, he would transfer his practical joking to another section of the ship.

At least, that's the way Cherry hoped that the Old Man was thinking.

To put Ziggy on guard against a night marauder would be disastrous. They would have to tell him what was in the sealed package. Knowing the conscientious little purser's reputation as a faithful employee of long-standing, Cherry felt sure that if he knew the package contained priceless *ambre blanc,* he would immediately report his own and Waidler's negligence to the captain. His conscience was bothering him enough as it was. That was why he had written that letter to Mr. Camelot as soon as he discovered his oversight in failing to turn the trivial toilet articles in to the home office.

Cherry could hardly eat a mouthful of her dinner. Brownie chattered on and on, full of Christmas Eve excitement. A cable of birthday greetings from the Spencer Club, that was delivered during dessert, did not help to cheer Cherry up much. Brownie, bubbling with curiosity, had to hear all about the Spencer Club. Unashamedly she hinted for an invitation to dinner at the Greenwich Village apartment while the ship was in the Port of New York.

Cherry, as heartily as possible, issued the invitation and then broke away.

Kirk Monroe stopped her in the corridor outside the grill. "Why so glum?" he asked. "Is it because you didn't get any birthday presents?" He slipped a tiny enameled pin into her hand. It was a lovely little miniature of the *Julita* plowing through a bit of the bright blue Caribbean.

"Strictly government issue," he admitted, grinning. "Christmas souvenirs for the passengers' dinner party tomorrow. But I thought you ought to have one today."

Cherry promptly pinned it on her uniform. "It's darling," she said, smiling.

"How goes the Mystery of the Missing Ambergris?" he demanded. "Did Jan cable the lawyer?"

Cherry nodded. As they walked down to B deck, she was tempted to follow the rules and regulations to the letter and dump the full responsibility of Jan's problem on the ship's surgeon's broad shoulders.

But that wouldn't be fair. The young physician's brilliant future must not be clouded by a shipboard scandal.

In Timmy's cabin, Kirk Monroe quickly scanned the bedside notes Cherry had taught Mrs. Crane how to keep. Then he gave the little boy a thorough examination. "Let's see," he said thoughtfully. "No fever for the last twenty-four hours. He's been normal really longer than that because we can discount the 101 he ran last evening. So we'll stop his sulfa with the eight o'clock dose."

Mrs. Crane, in a lovely taffeta frock, said gratefully, "Thank goodness. Then I don't have to get him up at four tomorrow morning?"

The young doctor smiled at her. "If he's normal in the morning, we'll stop taking his temperature altogether. I see no reason why he shouldn't play quietly around the pool Christmas afternoon."

Timmy, who had asked Santa for an endless number of rubber toys, bounced up and down with glee. Mrs. Crane hurried away to dinner. Just before the doctor left he said to Cherry:

"You might give him one last inhalation now, for good measure. And see that he doesn't get overstimulated tonight, if possible. It'll just start him coughing again, you know. He should be in bed at nine."

Cherry nodded and plugged in the vaporizer. Around eight-thirty Jan came into the room.

"I'm too nervous to eat," she said. "But one consolation is that Mother never felt better. I guess my dutiful-daughter act is having the desired effect." She sat down on the empty twin bed. "Have you thought of anything? *My* mind just goes around in circles."

"So does mine," Cherry admitted ruefully. "But we still have until Timmy's bedtime."

Tim poked his nose out from under his tent. "What have you got till my bedtime?"

"It's a secret." Cherry firmly tucked him back into the tent.

"Henry and I have a secret too," came Timmy's muffled voice.

"Oh, you have?" Jan sat up abruptly. "What kind of secret, Timmy?"

"It's a Christmas secret," Timmy told her. "Like all the presents under my bed. I'm going to stay awake all night and open every one of them, 'cept one, early in the morning, long before Mummy wakes up."

Cherry unplugged the vaporizer and put away the sheet and umbrella. "You won't need your tent anymore, Tim. Unless you want to make one yourself for fun."

Then Mrs. Crane arrived with Henry Landgraf. Timmy held up his arms:

"Hello, Henry Llama. Giddy-ap, giddy-ap."

With Timmy on his back, Mr. Landgraf led the way up to the library. Cherry thought she had never seen a more beautiful tree. It was silvered with icicles and lighted with nothing but huge, blue electric bulbs. But Tim was disappointed and said so in a voice so loud the captain must have heard it in his cabin:

"What kind of Christmas tree is that? There aren't any *red* balls on it. Who ever heard of a blue Christmas tree?" He buried his face in Henry's neck and sobbed.

Mrs. Crane fluttered her hands helplessly. "Oh, dear, what on earth shall we do? The poor lamb has been looking forward to this moment ever since he got sick."

And then Waidler, who had been watching the little group from the sidelines, moved closer. "Perhaps it might be wise if you went down to your cabin for a minute, Miss Cherry," he said. "I don't like to be the one to ruin a surprise, but the little boy is so upset . . ."

Cherry stared at him. "A surprise? In my stateroom?"

Something like a grin flickered across Waidler's weather-beaten features. "Your mother. She arranged it with me the afternoon before we sailed. The nicest little tree you ever saw. All red and gold balls and tinsel. A real old-fashioned tree. Not like that modernistic thing over there."

Cherry was already racing out of the library. Did anyone ever have such a thoughtful mother? A tree for Cherry's very own Christmas Eve! A red-and-gold tree. The kind Timmy liked!

Sure enough, when Cherry burst into her cabin, there it was, right smack in the middle of the floor. And around it were five odd-shaped packages: Cherry's "stocking presents."

Waidler was right behind her. "Thought we might set it up in the Crane suite just for tonight. An extra surprise for Timmy, when he comes back. Poor little fellow. Guess he's never had a real, homelike, old-fashioned Christmas."

Then Jan arrived, puffing indignantly. "Why on earth did you dash away like that, Cherry Ames? Oh! What a darling little tree."

Cherry quickly explained. "We're going to set it up in Timmy's room for tonight. He was so disappointed in the big blue-and-silver tree."

"I'll help," Jan offered. "Be *careful,* Waidy," she added as the steward reached for the green-and-red stand. "You almost tipped it over. Here, let *me* carry it."

Waidler grumbled, "Been toting Christmas trees for forty years and never tipped one over yet."

While Cherry watched amusedly they argued and finally arrived at a compromise. Waidy would carry the tree, but he would have to walk slowly so that Jan could keep a sharp eye on the ornaments.

So it was some time before the tree was finally placed to the satisfaction of all beside Timmy's bed.

Cherry noticed worriedly out of the corner of one eye that it was ten minutes past Timmy's bedtime when they returned to the library. The charming paneled room was filled with the after-dinner crowd now. Card tables had been set up in cozy corners; stewards were serving after-dinner coffee on low tables in front of the pale-yellow and green sofas.

But there was no sign of Timmy and his mother. Or of Timmy's "llama."

"They've gone on to the living room," Cherry guessed. "To hang up Timmy's stocking."

Jan led the way now, her full ballerina skirt billowing behind her. "Oh, Cherry," she breathed, "we weren't going to lose sight of Henry Landgraf for one minute. Remember?"

Cherry remembered all too well. She also remembered that punctual Ziggy retired on the dot of nine. And it was now nine-fifteen!

The living room was so crowded Cherry felt sure that all two hundred and twenty-five of the passengers had congregated there at once. They were grouped around the piano, singing carols. They milled in front of the fireplace, exchanging small gifts and strewing the hearth with colorful paper and tinsel ribbon. They blocked both the entrances, laughing and shouting greetings.

At last Cherry caught a glimpse of two little red stockings hanging from the mantel. Their tiny silver bells winked at her in the reflection of the light from the electric logs. Timmy had already hung up his stocking and Fuzzy's.

She had to raise her voice to make Jan hear her above the din and confusion. "They've gone back to the suite. Come on. *Hurry!*"

Breathlessly they pushed their way out into the corridor. Down the stairs they ran, side by side, Cherry momentarily forgetting that she was in uniform. Then they could hear Tim's laughter and crows of delight from the open door of his bedroom.

With a sigh of relief, Cherry saw that Henry Landgraf was still among those present. Mrs. Crane was in the other room chatting with guests she had invited down for after-dinner coffee. But Mr. Landgraf was sitting on Timmy's bed with Timmy on his lap. His bright blue eyes swept over the flushed faces of the girls in the doorway. He said to Cherry coolly:

"It was nice of you to donate a little red tree to such a good cause. We were reading the tag just now. A surprise from your mother?"

And then another cool voice, this time from the corridor behind Cherry, said:

"Nurse, please go to the refrigerator for penicillin."

Dazedly, Cherry whirled around. Dr. Monroe was just coming out of the dispensary. He said with worried abstraction:

"A petty officer cut himself rather badly yesterday and did not report the injury. I've already dressed the wound, but I'd like to give him a penicillin injection at once. The patient is in my office."

He disappeared into the door beyond the dispensary.

Cherry started off again for A deck. Jan followed her to the foot of the stairs:

"I'll keep an eye on our pirate until you get back. He won't get out of my sight for one minute."

Cherry unlocked the door to the purser's office and reached in to turn on the overhead lights. Some sixth sense made her go straight to the deep bottom drawer of the desk. She tugged it gently and it slid out as easily as though she had said, "Open, Sesame."

The lock had already been picked—or, a master key had been used to open it.

There were no telltale scratches on the wood or metal of the drawer. Cherry took one swift glance at the neat file of labeled envelopes and sealed packages. One of them stood out like a sore thumb. The label read:

"Paulding, Benedict, deceased. Cabin 141."

And the date was the Tuesday when the *Julita* had last stopped at the port of Willemstad.

Stunned and relieved, Cherry slammed the drawer shut. Then she heard the click of the automatic lock. Was the answer simply that Ziggy had neglected to shut it tightly enough when he closed up his desk at nine? All she could do was hope.

Snatching up the small bottle of penicillin, she turned off the lights and locked the door behind her. As she hurried down to the doctor's office, she couldn't help thinking of Henry Landgraf's strong, deft fingers, his cocksure, swaggering gait, his cold, blue eyes. Had he had time while she and Jan were arranging Timmy's tree to unseal that package, remove the milk-of-magnesia bottle, and reseal it?

Dr. Monroe, more relaxed now, said: "Thanks, Miss Ames. I'll give the injection myself. Tim Crane's been calling for you. Won't go to sleep until he's told you good night."

Cherry swiftly slipped into Timmy's bedroom which was only dimly lighted now. There was no sign of Henry or Jan, but she could hear Mrs. Crane's happy laughter floating through the half-open door to the living room of the suite.

Timmy, exhausted by too much excitement and the agony of anticipating what Santa would bring him, cried fretfully:

"I won't go to sleep till I open just one present. Just one present, Cherry. *Please!*"

"I'll have to ask your mother," Cherry said. Oh, where were Jan and Henry? Was impulsive Jan in trouble?

She opened the door to the living room a crack wider and then let out a long sigh. Sitting on the sofa, talking animatedly to an apparently completely captivated Henry Landgraf, was Jan Paulding! Sitting on his left, vying for the attractive "pirate's" attention, was Timmy's mother.

Mrs. Crane arose when Cherry caught her eye, and came to the door.

"Is it all right if Timmy opens one present tonight?" Cherry asked. "And hadn't you better lock the door to the corridor when I leave? I found it wide open."

Mrs. Crane flushed. "I did lock it once. He must have gotten out of bed and opened it himself. He wanted to be sure of catching you when you passed on your way to the doctor's office. And, of course, he may open one present."

Timmy, who had been listening, bounced up and down with joy. "Open your mouth and shut your eyes, Cherry," he ordered. "Then reach under the bed and pick out a present."

Cherry did as she was told and produced a small package. It was wrapped in thin, white tissue paper, held together in two places with Santa Claus stickers. But it was not tied with string and there was no card on it. Cherry said tiredly:

"I don't know who gave you this, but let's open it anyway."

Timmy peered at the package in the dim light. "It *has* to have a tag, Cherry. *All* Christmas presents have tags."

Cherry, thinking that the donor perhaps had written his name on the white tissue wrapping itself, held the package close to the bulb in Timmy's bedside lamp. Magically, the white paper took on a bluish tinge, and three large, printed words leaped into sight:

MILK OF MAGNESIA!

CHAPTER XVIII

Christmas Jugglery

TOO LATE, TIMMY YELLED:

"Oh, I forgot, Cherry. We can't open *that* present. *I* can't even open it tomorrow. That's our secret. Henry's and mine. It's Henry's very own Christmas present, but it got lonely in his cabin, so after we hung up my stocking we put it under the bed with all my presents. Henry's going to come in early as anything tomorrow morning and open it when I open mine."

"I bet he'll come in *early*," Cherry thought grimly. "And with quick sleight of hand he'll substitute another similarly wrapped package for this one."

Cherry herself did a swift juggling act then. With one hand she pushed the gift-wrapped milk-of-magnesia bottle down the floor to the very end of Timmy's bed. At the same time she snatched up another present and handed it to Timmy.

"Let's see what's in this one," she said, trying to sound calm and collected.

While Timmy yanked the red ribbon into hopeless knots, and tore the colorful paper into shreds, she said:

"Wait a minute. I've got some lonely presents in my cabin too. I'd like to open one of them with you right now."

"Okey-dokey." Tim grinned. "But *hurry.*"

Cherry hurried—so much so that she stumbled at the foot of Timmy's bed. When she lurched to her feet she was clutching in the folds of her uniform skirt "Henry's lonely gift."

Then, as though on wings, she flew down the corridor to her own cabin. She remembered that one of her "stocking" presents had looked like a pint-size bottle of perfume. It was undoubtedly something with an impossible odor—a joke from Charlie.

But it was even better than that. It was a bottle of cheap, powdered bath salts! "Carrying coals to Newcastle," the card read. Cherry snatched a tiny enamel funnel from her nurse's kit. It took but a minute to transfer the exotic-smelling ambergris to her hot water bag and fill the milk-of-magnesia bottle with gardenia bath salts.

Henry, thank goodness, had licked his Santa Claus stickers so hastily there was still plenty of glue left. When Cherry had finished rewrapping the blue pint bottle no one would ever have known it had been tampered with.

"Two can play at this game," she said, chuckling inwardly. "Maybe I can't pick locks as expertly as he can, but I can unseal and reseal packages even better!"

She could see it all now: Mrs. Crane caught up by a group of her friends as she and Henry, with Timmy on his back, pushed their way into the crowded living room; Timmy hanging up the two red stockings but refusing to go to bed on the dot of nine; Henry saying indulgently:

"All right, Tim. You wait here in front of the fireplace while I go get my lonely present."

But instead of going to his cabin he had strolled diagonally across the corridor to the purser's office. Nobody in that milling Christmas crowd would have noticed that he was inserting his master key into the door of the office, not his stateroom.

Then those strong, deft fingers had worked swiftly but surely on the desk lock and the sealed package. Before coming to Timmy's cabin earlier he had, of course, tucked tissue paper and stickers in one pocket of his gabardine suit, and a bottle of real milk of magnesia in the other. Tomorrow one of the passengers would discover his or her loss. But there would be no hue and cry about that—a clumsy maid had, of course, broken it while dusting.

Henry, with his master key—or *keys*—had indeed been master of the situation. He had made but one error and Cherry had played right into his hands. In his haste to get back to Timmy before the little boy made a scene, he had not slammed the desk drawer quite hard enough.

But it didn't matter now. Because *Cherry* was now mistress of the situation.

Timmy, busy with a box of cardboard pirates, did not notice when Cherry slipped a package under his bed. He said without much enthusiasm:

"Open your present, Cherry. I'll bet *you* didn't get pirates."

Cherry had brought along Dr. Joe's "stocking" gift too. It was a child's doctor's kit, complete with stethoscope, wooden thermometer, and tiny forceps. Timmy immediately pounced upon it. Expertly he hung the toy stethoscope around his neck and shook down the thermometer.

Cherry laughed. "It's my Christmas Eve present to you, Timmy. And now you must go to sleep."

Obediently, he nestled under the covers, pirates, stethoscope, and all. Cherry tucked him in and laid her cheek against his for a minute as he sleepily mumbled his prayers:

"God bless Mummy, God bless Daddy, God bless Henry, God bless Cherry—" He was sound asleep.

"God bless *you*, 'Tiny Tim,' " Cherry whispered as she tiptoed out of the room. "If it hadn't been for you, we never would have found Jan's ambergris."

Cherry slept with her hot-water bottle under her pillow. She dreamed happily of ferocious pirates who, decked in *leis* of gardenias, danced around the tall blue and silver Christmas tree. Sometimes they wore Santa Claus masks and sometimes they twirled long, black mustachios, but they were, each and every one, Henry Landgraf.

She awoke to the sound of loud knocking and shouts of "Merry Christmas, Sleepyhead. Merry Christmas!"

It was Brownie, proudly displaying a wrist watch from her parents and a lovely little friendship ring from, as she said, "My very best boy friend."

Cherry opened her other "stocking" presents then: A tiny celluloid octopus from Midge—Timmy would enjoy that in the pool. A miniature plum pudding from her mother, and a cardboard stocking full of candied cherries from Dad. "Sweets to the Sweet," he had written.

Cherry promptly succumbed to another wave of homesickness. Tears welled up into her dark-brown eyes. Cherry blinked them back, laughing at herself. Brownie, scraping one index finger across the other, hooted:

"Sissy for shame, Cherry Ames. You're a big girl now." She snatched up the pillow and tossed it at Cherry. And there, in plain view, was the red hot water bottle. Brownie gasped. "For goodness sake, Cherry. What on earth were you doing with *that* last night? It was as hot as anything in my cabin. The air conditioning wasn't working properly." She reached for the rubber bag, but Cherry snatched it away just in time.

"I had a toothache," she fibbed nonchalantly, and carried the hot water bottle across the room to toss it up on the top shelf of her closet.

Brownie, admiring her new ring and wrist watch, said vaguely, "Thought you put an ice bag on your face when you had a toothache."

"Sometimes you do," Cherry admitted. "Sometimes heat is the only thing that helps."

Brownie yawned. "Well, I'd better scramble into uniform and get up on A deck. It's Christmas for the passengers, but it's just one more day to us poor slaves."

Cherry celebrated by taking a hot saltwater shower. She took the hot water bottle into the glassed-in compartment with her. She was not going to let that little rubber bag out of her sight until she had delivered it in person to Jan Paulding. After that it was no longer Cherry's responsibility. Jan could turn it over to the captain until the ship docked the next day in Willemstad. Jan could have Henry Landgraf arrested, if she liked.

But Cherry doubted if Jan would do that. From the glimpse she had caught of them chatting together the evening before, in the Crane suite, they were now as thick as thieves.

And Henry? When he took one whiff of those violent "gardenia" bath salts, he would know that although he had played his cards close, poker-faced throughout, Lady Luck, in the form of Tim Crane, had deserted him.

Would he throw down his cards now and admit defeat? Or would he deal another hand? Time was running out. He had but one more day and one more night. Even he would have no way of knowing that the precious *ambre blanc* was now shifting around inside the hot water bottle of the ship's nurse.

Cherry slipped into her uniform and was just pinning on her cap when someone tapped on her door. For a moment she was frightened. Was it Timmy's pirate? Had he somehow discovered her juggling act of the night before?

The other occupants of the women's crew quarters had already gone off to their duties. Cherry was alone in her cabin in the dim, narrow passageway off the main corridor. It would be inviting disaster to open her door. And then, frozen with horror, she remembered that she had not locked it when she came back from her shower.

The only thing to do was to brazen it out. Cherry squared her shoulders and said in a clear voice:

"Come in."

It was Jan! She had flung a seersucker bathrobe over her pajamas. Cherry threw her arms around the tall young girl and cried hilariously, "Merry Christmas, darling. A very merry Christmas!"

Jan hugged Cherry and said, "I guess it's just about the merriest Christmas I ever had. Oh, Cherry, I can hardly believe it. I'm going to college after all."

Cherry stared at her in amazement. How could Jan know that her precious ambergris was safe and sound? Before she could get out a word, Jan went on ecstatically.

"I don't care if he is a—well, a shady character. He's so *gallant*, Cherry. After we left the Cranes' last night I invited him in to our suite. I wasn't going to let him out of my sight, remember? Mother is simply wild about him. She hung on every word he said. And then it came out that I was Uncle Benedict's niece, and just as I thought, he's Uncle Ben's ex-partner."

Cherry managed a weak: "Oh? Then what?"

"Well, then nothing much," Jan admitted. "Not last night, anyway. We talked about everything but ambergris, of course. And he told us the most fascinating stories about some of the fantastic adventures he and Uncle Ben had had in all the most foreign spots in the world. He called him 'Uncle Ben' too, you see, and really thought of him as an uncle, because Henry hasn't any family of his own. And until Mother and I told him, he thought Uncle Ben didn't have any nephews or nieces. He read in the newspaper, stories when Uncle died, about his prominent brothers and sisters, but there wasn't any mention of *me*."

Jan, her hazel eyes glowing, began to pace up and down the tiny cabin. "Don't you see, Cherry? I know now that he was after that ambergris too, but he felt it *belonged* to him. After all, my uncle practically adopted Henry about sixteen years ago when he was only twenty-two. He was in some sort of trouble with the French police and Uncle Ben rescued him." Jan dimpled. "Henry says the 'trouble' was simply that he couldn't speak French then, but I'll bet it was not quite so simple as that."

"There we see eye to eye, Jan Paulding," Cherry muttered. "My guess is that the 'trouble' had something to do with breaking and entering. He may have reformed after Uncle Ben 'adopted' him, but he hasn't forgotten any of his old tricks."

But Jan wasn't listening. "Those blue, blue eyes of his! They're as blue as the Caribbean Sea."

"And just as hypnotic," Cherry mumbled.

Jan laughed. "That's right. Anyway, he didn't leave until midnight, and then it was Christmas. And I just *knew* anybody as gallant as that wouldn't steal anything on Christmas Day, Cherry."

"Christmas Day or Christmas Eve," Cherry said tartly, "it's all the same thing. And he did steal your ambergris, Jan."

"I know." Jan shrugged. "But you can't call it stealing. Not really, Cherry."

Cherry gasped. Was Jan going to do a complete right-about-face of character and go sentimental? Hypnotized, was she going to let Henry Landgraf keep the ambergris simply because he had felt *he* was her uncle's rightful heir?

Cherry's mind reeled. And how in the world did Jan know that the ambergris had been stolen?

Jan herself answered that question. "Don't look so shocked, Cherry. He only did it as a Christmas surprise for me. Honestly, you could have knocked me over with a feather when Waidy arrived this morning with that package.

" 'Merry Christmas, Miss Jan,' he said. 'Compliments of Mr. Landgraf.' And then when I tore off the paper and saw that milk-of-magnesia bottle, I just tucked it in my bathrobe pocket and came racing down here to you."

With a flourish, Jan produced from her bathrobe pocket a cloudy blue bottle. The very one Cherry had filled with Charlie's bath salts on Christmas Eve! Jan unscrewed the top and then she wrinkled up her dainty nose.

"Oh, Cherry," she wailed, "this isn't ambergris! It hasn't got a delicate fragrance at all. It's more like that ghastly perfume you have to breathe on crowded buses." She crumpled down on Cherry's bunk and burst into tears. "That horrid man! He's played a trick on me."

Jan did not spend much time in idle tears. She was angry, indignant, chagrined. Jumping from Cherry's bed with clenched fists, she moaned, "Oh, what a miserable fool I've been! I let him soft soap me into thinking him a romantic pirate with a heart of gold. And then—then—!"

The young girl now was pacing up and down within the narrow confines of Cherry's stateroom. She kept clenching and unclenching her hands, striking one tight fist against the other.

"What does he think I am—a child?" she raged. "Does he think I don't know the difference between dimestore junk and real ambergris? That cold-blooded thief wasn't satisfied to steal what was going to pay for my education—what he knew my uncle whom he professed to idolize had left for me—but then he tried to make me think he had restored it to me as a Christmas present—"

Cherry made an effort to calm the girl's violence. "Jan," she cried, "stop it! You'll make yourself sick. Calm down! Your precious ambergris is safe—"

But Jan wasn't listening. She continued her tirade. Her voice rose almost to a scream.

"He's the meanest man in the world! He would steal pennies from a poor box and then slip a note in their place 'blessed are the poor.' I'm going to the captain and I'm going to have Henry Landgraf exposed for the miserable sneak thief he is. Oh, I wish I knew—"

Cherry had had enough of Jan Paulding's hysterical outburst. She arose and putting her two hands firmly on the girl's shoulders, forced her down to a sitting position on her bed.

"That's enough, Jan! You've had your big scene. Now you are going to hear what I've been trying to tell you ever since you came into my stateroom. I'm glad you're over your schoolgirl crush on this highhanded young man. What I tried to tell you was that your ambergris is safe."

Then, having quieted the trembling young girl, Cherry told her of last night's adventures. Jan listened, wide-eyed, without interruption.

"So you see," concluded the smiling cruise nurse, "you've got nothing to worry about, darling. I have your ambergris safe and sound. See? It's right here in my hot water bottle. Take a whiff and prove it for yourself."

Cherry unscrewed the top of her hot water bottle and held it under Jan's nose. One sniff was all she needed. With a glad cry she hugged Cherry until the latter cried, "Stop, you're bashing in my ribs!"

"You're a wonder, Cherry," said Jan, her voice deep with emotion. "I'll be grateful to you all my life. How wonderful that you were able to beat Henry Landgraf at his own game. What are we going to do now—go to the captain?"

Cherry thought a minute. "For the present," she said, "I believe we ought to leave the ambergris right there in my hot water bottle. You run along now, dear, and try to act as though you had the stuff in the bottle just as Mr. Hijacker Landgraf gave it to you. A Merry Christmas, Jan!"

Jan stooped and planted a kiss on one of Cherry's red cheeks, then darted away, slamming the door behind her. Cherry stood stock-still for a minute, then she slowly went over and locked the door. The ambergris, she realized now, was *not* safe in her hot water bottle— not as long as Henry Landgraf remained aboard the *Julita*. She doubted if it would be safe anywhere on the ship—in the purser's safe, even in the captain's cabin—now that the thief knew that someone had switched the contents of that milk-of-magnesia bottle which he had slipped under Timmy's bed.

He would start searching again, of course. Clever questioning of Timmy would lead Mr. Henry Landgraf straight to the door of the ship's nurse's cabin. And after that her office and then the dispensary. There probably wasn't a spot he would overlook.

Quickly Cherry made up her mind. There was no time to lose. Taking the hot water bottle she hung it casually from one of the shower valves where it looked about as conspicuous as the soap dish.

After breakfast she sent Merry Christmas radiograms to her family and the Spencer Club. What a story she would have to tell them after this cruise! Midge's eyes would probably pop right out of her head, and Charlie just wouldn't believe a word of it. Neither would Gwen. Cherry could almost hear her sniff: "That's enough, Ames! You read that yarn in your little patient's pirate book."

And then Cherry thought of Timmy—*and* the one perfect place to hide the precious *ambre blanc*. There was just one place on the whole ship where Mr. Henry Landgraf *wouldn't* look. Simply because he had already searched it carefully—the drawer in the Crane suite which was crammed full with Timmy's toys!

Timmy, Cherry felt sure, would spurn those toys now that Santa Claus had brought him so many new ones. He probably wouldn't even open that drawer until his new Christmas presents had lost their charm.

Mrs. Crane greeted Cherry with: "Merry Christmas, dear. Tim has a present for you. Please excuse me, but I'm late for breakfast."

Timmy, almost lost under billowing waves of Christmas wrappings, scrabbled around and finally came up with a thick, square box. He yelled, "I know what it is, but I won't tell. I never tell secrets." He thrust the box behind him impishly. "You've got to guess, Cherry. I won't give it to you 'less you do."

Cherry laughed and said to Mrs. Crane, "You shouldn't have bought me a present, but it was awfully sweet of you just the same."

"It's twin presents 'cause you had a birthday yesterday," Timmy interrupted, "and it's red and very fuzzy-wuzzy."

"I give up," Cherry sighed. "Unless it's a red Teddy bear."

Tim let her open it then. Nestling in the tissue-lined box, bearing the label of the ship's little novelty shop, were two lovely angora wool sweaters; one with short sleeves, its twin a cardigan.

Cherry was so pleased she could only stutter her thanks. But as she tucked the scarlet sweaters back in the box, her eyes fell upon the abandoned and neglected Fuzzy-Wuzzy on the floor.

Timmy was saying proudly, "Mummy bought 'em last night. But I didn't tell anybody what was in that box—not even Henry, or Waidy or Jan or Kirk. I always keep secrets."

As he finished speaking in his piping voice, he dived under the bedcovers. Quickly Cherry crossed the stateroom and picked up the battered panda. Lifting the lid of the sweater box she buried Fuzzy-Wuzzy under the sweaters and hastily replaced the cover. It was not an instant too soon, for Timmy was emerging from the covers.

With a hurried "Back in a minute, Tim," Cherry sped to her room. Behind the locked door she went feverishly to work. Quickly she ripped the seam of Fuzzy-Wuzzy and removed most of the wadding. In its place went the red-rubber hot water bottle with its precious contents. Then with needle and thread Fuzzy-Wuzzy's yawning incision was sewed up again. She hefted the panda critically. Was it heavier than it had been before? It seemed about the same.

Then Cherry took the sweaters out of the gift box and put Fuzzy-Wuzzy in their place. A moment later, when she stepped into the Crane suite everything was quiet. Timmy, still surrounded by his new toys and their wrappings, had fallen asleep. Mrs. Crane had not returned.

Trembling in her haste, Cherry took Fuzzy-Wuzzy out of the box. Then opening the toy drawer she pushed him back among Timmy's abandoned toys. With a deep sigh of relief she sank quietly into a chair by the bedside of the little boy.

Timmy opened one sleepy eye. Seeing Cherry there, the cardboard gift box in her arms, he was awake and sitting up instantly.

"Cherry," he piped, "what do you think Henry got for Christmas?"

"What did Henry get?" she asked with more curiosity than she dared show.

Timmy shouted at the top of his lungs: "Yo, ho, ho, a bottle of bay rum! It's made from bayberry leaves and *they* grow in the West Indies, Cherry. *Also,* tomorrow we're going to be in the West Indies. *And* Henry's going to take me ashore and show me where that Peter man's leg is 'posed to be buried." He stopped suddenly and then finished with:

"Aren't you, Henry?"

Cherry jumped and whirled in the direction toward which Timmy was looking. Standing just inside the open French doors, a bland mask on his strong, tanned face, was Henry Landgraf. But to Cherry he might just as well have had a bandanna tied around his head and gold rings dangling from his ears.

"Merry Christmas, Miss Cherry," he boomed in that deep, rather harsh voice of his. "Was Santa good to you?" he continued, eying the box on Cherry's lap.

"Very good, thank you," Cherry said with more emphasis perhaps than was necessary. Something flickered in his bright blue eyes, and Cherry *knew* that he knew who had substituted the bath salts for the stolen ambergris.

Both hands were in his pockets as he swaggered into the room. For one wild moment Cherry felt like screaming. Would a pistol suddenly emerge from one of those pockets?

"Don't be a complete fool, Ames," she scolded herself. "He doesn't play the game that way. And he would never in this world do anything to frighten Timmy."

A clenched brown fist came out of one pocket. Then something small and hard dropped into Cherry's lap beside the sweater box. She looked down and saw a tiny bottle of fabulously expensive, imported perfume.

"A little souvenir of the—er joke we've enjoyed together," he said easily. "I leave the ship at Curaçao tomorrow."

Before Cherry could utter a word, he had strolled out of the room. From the deck came his mocking farewell: "There's not much ambergris in that. But enough so you'll remember me for a while."

Timmy struggled out of the bedclothes. "Don't forget tomorrow, Henry," he piped. But Henry did not answer.

Cherry stared down at the gilt crown stopper on the tiny, amber bottle. He had dropped it in her lap as a token of his respect for the part she had played in their duel of wits. It was the gallant and perhaps mocking gesture of one who could be a good loser when he had to be.

It occurred to Cherry that Henry Landgraf had not sent Jan that bottle of bath salts altogether as a cruel joke. It was also a cryptic but unmistakable message to Cherry herself—telling her he knew she had the ambergris and also knew she would restore it to its rightful owner. What was more, he was counting on Cherry to keep the secret—in order to protect the purser and the steward. There was nerve for you!

Henry, eavesdropping outside the Paulding suite the afternoon before, must have heard Cherry beg Jan not to report the matter to the captain for Ziggy's and Waidler's sake. So now he coolly was depending on Cherry's loyalty to her friends to enable him to get off scot free.

The door into the corridor opened. Mrs. Crane had returned from her breakfast. Cherry arose, bidding goodbye to Timmy and his mother, and started down the corridor. She walked slowly for once, feeling curiously exhausted.

Could it be possible that this still was Christmas morning? So much had happened! And the end was not yet. Tomorrow they would dock at Willemstad. There would be airmail letters awaiting her. Midge had hinted that there would be so many Cherry would need a truck. She could hardly wait to hear the latest news of her family and friends.

She looked forward to a sightseeing and shopping tour with Brownie—a swim at Piscadera Bay—perhaps a visit with Jan to the property she had inherited from her uncle which was to launch the young girl on her chosen career. . .

"Why so pensive this morning, Cherry?" Kirk Monroe's voice broke into her thoughts as the young doctor fell in step with her down the corridor.

Startled, Cherry smiled up at him.

"I'm not, really, Kirk," she replied, "at least, I don't think so—but I have lots of things to tell you."

"Come on, let's go up to the grill," Dr. Monroe suggested, taking Cherry's arm. "We can both use another cup of coffee."

In the nearly deserted grill Cherry related everything that had happened since the night before.

"Of course, I'm delighted that Jan's ambergris is safe at last," she finished, "but, somehow, Kirk, when anyone is such a good loser . . ."

"Maybe Henry Landgraf is a good loser, Cherry, and *maybe* he's a good actor," Kirk Monroe pointed out grimly. "You know now that the man's a thief; but you can only hope that he has admitted defeat." The young doctor stood up abruptly. "We have to think of the other passengers, Cherry. We have no choice now. I'll have to report this whole thing to the captain."

CHAPTER XIX

Happy Ending

IT WAS SNOWING THAT WEDNESDAY AFTER NEW YEAR'S when the *Julita* steamed into New York harbor. The big white flakes seemed to be drifting horizontally instead of falling vertically. To Cherry Ames and Kirk Monroe, standing at the rail waiting to catch a glimpse of the city's towers through the snowstorm, it did not seem possible that only a few days ago the skies had been blue and the air soft and all of the passengers and crew in their summer whites.

And now Cherry found herself shivering slightly in her chocolate-brown suit and her poinsettia-red hat as she leaned against the icy rail.

"I'm crazy about that perfume you're wearing," Kirk was saying. "What is it?"

"It was a present from a pirate," Cherry replied. "He hoped it would make me remember him." She smiled up at Kirk. "Oh, I'll remember him all right, down to the last drop of his farewell present."

Kirk grinned. "I'm jealous. Timmy's pirate was in many ways a likable dog, if he'd only had more respect for other people's property."

Cherry seemed to be lost in thought for several moments. "I'll never forget that morning at Curaçao. Timmy and I were at the rail watching the pontoon bridge swing open at Willemstad. Suddenly there was a step behind us. We both turned. It was Henry Landgraf. He was in shirt sleeves and wearing sneakers. I never was as surprised in my life—especially after the captain's telling us the night before that Henry would be kept in the brig until he could be turned over to the port officer at Curaçao."

"No brig ever was built that could hold that one," the doctor replied.

"He didn't look at me, not once. But when Timmy let out a squeal of delight, he stopped, reached into his pocket, pulled out an old Spanish coin, and handed it to Tim. 'Something to remember our days on the Spanish Main, Tim,' he said—"

"A pirate to the end," murmured Kirk. "That was probably a Spanish piece of eight."

"A moment later," continued Cherry, "he had climbed over the rail and dived into the canal. Timmy screamed like a banshee. Everybody rushed to the rail to see Henry swimming for the nearest dock. I doubt whether the *Julita* ever made a more exciting entrance."

A few hours later, Cherry and Kirk were sitting in a Village restaurant only a few blocks from No. 9.

Over a bowl of hot soup Cherry said thoughtfully, "I keep thinking about Timmy's pirate. I know that he picked locks and broke and entered and took something that didn't belong to him. But I can't help hoping that—that he got away. Prison would kill something in a man like that. After all, Jan got her inheritance—"

Kirk grinned. "Criminals are going to be in clover when you ladies take over the law courts," he said.

"Well, it all came out all right, didn't it? Ziggy and Waidler are still in the captain's good graces. And wasn't that Mr. Camelot a funny little fussbudget? How do you suppose a crusty old man like Jan's uncle could have put such trust in that dry little man?"

Kirk shook his head.

"I missed Jan on the trip back," Cherry said softly. "I'm going to miss that little Timmy, too. Who knows but I may find myself missing you, too, Kirk, even though you did scare me half to death that first day out."

Cherry knew that her cheeks matched her perky little red hat. She liked this serious young doctor and hoped that he wouldn't go out of her life forever when the *Julita* sailed again on Friday. She said with a trace of shyness, "Maybe you'll have time while you're in port to have dinner some evening at the Spencer Club. Bertha Larsen is a wonderful cook."

Kirk's gray eyes widened in mock horror. "You couldn't lure me to dinner with six nurses no matter how good a cook Bertha is." Then he sobered. "Besides, Cherry, I want you all to myself. I've got only two days. Have dinner with me tonight and tomorrow. Please."

Cherry laughed. "One would think we hadn't had breakfast, lunch, and dinner together nearly every day for the past twelve days!" Then she added, "Dinner tonight and tomorrow night would be fun, but you must meet the girls. They'd never forgive me. And besides, you'll like them and they'll like you."

"Compromise," Kirk said quickly. "I'll brave your den, but you'll have to go dancing with me both nights. Think of all those evenings at sea when we had to watch the passengers from the sidelines."

Cherry's eyes twinkled. "All right. But sometime let's go for a swim in one of the hotel pools." She told him then for the first time about her illegal dip on the *Julita*.

Kirk threw back his head and roared with laughter. "Cherry Ames," he chuckled, "you've got more spunk than any girl I ever knew! I've a good mind to give up my ship's surgeon job just to stay on shore near you. As a matter of fact," he added seriously, "I'm going to do just that in a month or so. One of the big New York children's hospitals has offered me a residency. I've just about decided to specialize in pediatrics."

"And you should," Cherry said with a smile. "The way you handled that imp, Timmy, was something to see."

He looked as pleased as though she had told him he was the best children's doctor in the world. "Maybe someday we'll end up in the same hospital," he said. "I'd like that. Would you, Cherry?"

Cherry nodded. "I'd like it very much."

And somehow she knew that although the cruise had come to a happy ending, her friendship with young Dr. Monroe had only just begun.